LOST BODIES

François Gantheret is a psychoanalyst. He has written both essays and short stories, but *Lost Bodies* is his first novel. He lives in Paris.

Euan Cameron's translations from the French include works by Julien Green, Simone de Beauvoir, Paul Morand, François Bizot and, most recently, Pierre Péju's new novel *Clara's Tale*.

FRANÇOIS GANTHERET

Lost Bodies

TRANSLATED FROM THE FRENCH BY

Euan Cameron

GIFT FROM MICHELLE

READ AUGUST 7 AND 8, 2009

VINTAGE BOOKS
London

Published by Vintage 2007

2 4 6 8 10 9 7 5 3 1

First published with the title *Les Corps perdus*
by Éditions Gallimard, Paris, 2004

First published in Great Britain in 2006 by
Harvill Secker
Random House, 20 Vauxhall Bridge Road, London SW1V 2SA

www.vintage-books.co.uk

Addresses for companies within The Random House Group Limited can be found at: www.randomhouse.co.uk/offices.htm

The Random House Group Limited Reg. No. 954009

A CIP catalogue record for this book
is available from the British Library

ISBN 9780099484974

This book is supported by the French Ministry of Foreign Affairs, as part of the Burgess programme run by the Cultural Department of the French Embassy in London

Liberté • Égalité • Fraternité
RÉPUBLIQUE FRANÇAISE

The Random House Group Limited makes every effort to ensure that the papers used in its books are made from trees that have been legally sourced from well-managed and credibly certified forests. Our paper procurement policy can be found at:
www.randomhouse.co.uk/paper.htm

FSC
Mixed Sources
Product group from well-managed forests and other controlled sources
www.fsc.org Cert no. TT-COC-2139
© 1996 Forest Stewardship Council

Printed in the by UK by CPI Bookmarque, Croydon, CR0 4TD

Lost Bodies

1

For some time now, he no longer slept. Eyes wide open in the darkness, he lay in wait. It was like this every morning. He had only a very hazy notion of what it meant: mornings for him were spent just keeping watch, waiting, sitting with his back to the wall, his legs folded and his arms around his knees, clenched to his chest so as to allow as little access as possible to the cold which was more acute at that time of day, his head thrown back, his eyes glued to the lid above him that was still not yet visible. In the icy night into which he had been cast, where he could not even see his hands, even though they were a few centimetres from his face, it would come, rising anew each time, a hope which never let him down and which kept him alive day after day. He would have liked to be able to pinpoint exactly when the apparition came, but that moment always eluded him. It was just there, it was there now, that thin sliver of light which delineated the rounded contours of the lid three metres above his head.

There was a time when he had kept count of these apparitions and had converted them into days, weeks, months. How long had he done this? He could not even remember when he had stopped doing so: it was lost in a night as thick as the one that had just dispersed up there. All that existed now was the miracle, unique each time, of this circle of brightness, so pale to begin with, but which grew in intensity more quickly than his eyes could endure, to the extent that he had to avert them from time to time, for a few seconds, before resuming his watch, fearing on each occasion that it might have disappeared while he was looking away. He realised how foolish this fear was – did anything here rely upon him? – yet he could not rid himself of the habit.

Up above, unperturbed, the light intensified

until it became incandescent, radiating into the hole and clinging to the rough edges of rock. At night it was only the cold biting into his flesh and gnawing at his muscles that prevented him from dissolving into the darkness. Now, in the half-light in which he could see his hands and his legs, he rediscovered himself, a man, Andrès, who had not forgotten his name, not yet. A man in stinking rags, hunched up at the bottom of a well two metres in diameter and four metres deep that was enclosed by a heavy wooden lid. Three large tin cans, on which the brand name of the vegetable oil they once contained could still be read, stood in a row in front of him, each of them fitted with a handle that had been added for his use. One, which was empty, was meant for his food; the second contained what was left of some murky water; the third, almost full, was for his excrement. Now, he had to wait for the second event of the day, at an unspecified time, when the lid would be raised and the cans changed, one after the other. Next . . . But he did not think about what was to happen next; there was only the waiting, the constant waiting, his eyes fixed on the circle of blazing light up there. When the tears came and his sight blurred, he lowered his head and gazed at the cans, then after a while he took up his watch once more. The lid, the cans, the lid, the cans . . . Waiting. Nothing else.

A pain in his knees revived a recent memory, a fear, a few thoughts: he must be ready. One morning – how long ago was it? – at the moment when the lid was opened and he had had to hook on the cans, the only movement he was required to make all day, his numb legs had given way beneath him. By the time he managed to get to his feet again, the lid had closed. That, especially, must never happen.

With the help of his hands, he slowly stood up, a sharp ache in his knees, his hips, his back. Once he was upright and leaning against the wall, he cautiously attempted to stretch his legs until the pain abated. For safety's sake, he decided to remain standing and to resume his routine again; the lid, the cans, the lid . . . and suddenly, without any warning, giving him a fright every time, there was the noise of the lid being removed and the explosion of blinding light. At the very moment that the hook, swinging on the end of the rope, and on which the handles of the cans had to be hung one after the other, reached the bottom of the well, his damaged eyes were full of tears and he could see nothing. Must not forget to pour out the remains of the water, so that it won't pollute what will be sent down to him. And try to keep the can full of excrement as far away as possible while he holds it, for the moment he let go it would knock against the wall and spill part of its contents in long trickles that stank until they were dry.

All this was done without a word being uttered. He was unable to see the person or people whose job it was to expedite this operation, only a blurred shadow that disrupted the dazzling brightness that fell from the sky. Sometimes there was a gob of spit, which he did not hurry to wipe off because he was almost grateful. One day he felt lukewarm water streaming down his face. It took a few seconds to realise that someone was urinating over him; he began to move away to avoid the spray that pursued him, then he stood still so that he could receive the last drop.

Then, with a dull thud that fell with the darkness into the well, the lid was put back in place and he needed time before he could make out the walls and the cans once more; time he spent standing upright, against the rock, his eyes closed and his arms pinned to his body, a time when death could well have seized its opportunity and would have been welcomed eagerly, but death preferred to wait and was probably gratified when he slowly reopened his eyes in his tomb.

Once his eyes had become accustomed to the dark again, there came a moment of utmost importance, a sequence of movements that mattered to him more than anything else, the one remnant of humanity that he had been able to preserve. He knelt down in front of the cans and did his best to ignore the insipid smell of the food; to shun it rather, to keep it at one remove. Carefully, he poured a little water into his cupped hands and lowered his head until he could bathe his face in his palms. He forced himself to open his eyelids so that his eyeballs could feel the coolness of the water. It was his soul that he was cleansing in this way, the most precious part of him, which he must protect and conserve at all costs; in this endless night it was a child he was bathing, a miracle of innocence that was still untouched.

Then, taking great care of the water that was left in his hands, he dabbed it lightly on his forehead, cheeks and neck. His beard had not grown as much as he feared, covering his face in a tight layer of curls that were so closely knit that even the water had difficulty reaching the skin of his cheeks. His hair, too, appeared to have stopped growing, and he was surprised to find that it had formed a thick helmet which he had to force apart with his fingers to reach his skull.

Less frequently, he took some water and spread it over his torso, his stomach, where his muscles felt like ropes, his penis, which had been inert and unused for so long that he had forgotten what desire was, his anus, too, and those parts that had been soiled by diarrhoea. And with the remaining moisture on his palms, he massaged his legs, on which the flesh seemed to have disappeared.

Only then did he turn towards the can half-filled with a thick soup that was always the same, filling his mouth in cupped handfuls and retaining contact for as long as possible with his tongue, his gums, his palate and the whole of his mouth, which in due course became the one satisfied cavity in his entire body. Then he swallowed, in small portions which he could feel as they went down inside him, tracing secret, forgotten passages that were rediscovered each time.

Occasionally, drowned in the liquid mass, he came across a more solid morsel: depending on its consistency it might be a vegetable, or even . . . he didn't think meat, but something animal. A part of an animal, a piece of gristle, or a stringy mass. Then, closing his eyes as if for some ritual, he chewed. Chewing was a rare pleasure. By chewing, he could awaken time and make it endure; he could impose the steady, sustained rhythm he required on this segment of animal that dwindled in the process, and which he made last as long as possible. It was a precious moment, the memory of which he retained for a long time afterwards.

He could eat only once during the daytime. The temperature rose very quickly inside the well, even though the walls conserved a degree of chill, and by evening anything that was left in the can had gone rotten or turned sour. Even the water had become murky and seemed contaminated. Feeding oneself remained the morning duty. Later, when he was lying on his side, huddled around his belly, seeking the cool of the earth beneath him, began the long, endless tunnel of daytime. One solitary thought, in order to survive in the stupor of the heat: evening always comes. There is always an end. Think only of that. Don't think.

2

Tamia gathers the folds of her woven woollen coat about her. The sun has already left the flank of the hill where she stands and the heat accumulated in the stones quickly disperses. The air becomes more transparent as it begins to freeze. Down below, the shadows of the rocky outcrop known as the *reg* lengthen in the angled light; a flow of grey-blue velvet descends, continually darkening. In the distance the peaks of the great dunes still glow, and the sharply defined ridges fade as a sombre liquid mass ascends their slopes. About 300 metres away, at the point where the hills subside, a few lights have been switched on in the fort. It consists of nothing but a group of three small, single-storey buildings, built around a large patch of waste ground dotted with evenly distributed circles and surrounded by a clay wall. The main gate, which gives on to the *reg*, is guarded by a small shack, where the first light was switched on. She can see two figures moving about inside, and a column of smoke climbing vertically into the still air.

A smaller gate at the back, made of wood, opens on to the hills. Two heaps of rubbish are stacked up outside. It is through here that the soldier will emerge shortly, once night has fallen.

She whistles softly, briskly, between her teeth, as her three goats, their udders swollen, cluster round, making a muffled sound with their hooves and trampling the ground. She sits down on a rock, the stone jar between her legs, and starts to milk the first one. Her two hands guide the teats towards the top of the jar with regular thrusts, one after the other, and the spray of frothy milk rings out with a clear sound that dies away as the vessel fills. The two other goats nudge her gently on either side, with friendly, impatient jerks of their heads.

By the time she has finished with the third

goat, night has engulfed the desert. The ridges of the mountains still stand out, black against the deep blue of the sunset. In a few minutes this sliver of the world shall itself have slipped away, and nothing will remain apart from the legion of cold stars that now fill the sky, into which she gazes distractedly for hours on end.

She lifts the rug that conceals her hiding-place, a tiny triangular space between two rocks, where she has to stoop to move around. She throws back her head and drinks a little of the tepid, frothy, fragrant-smelling milk straight from the jar before putting the container back in its exact place against the rock, her movements unerring in the pitch blackness, and covering it with a cloth which her hand knows exactly where to find. The rugs that make up her bed, the precious wineskin in which she keeps water, her supply of dates and flour, her hairbrush, the kohl for her eyes and the palm oil she smears on her skin, her carefully folded white linen tunic and, beneath her, the long knife that has been sharpened again and again, with its cold and deadly blade, which she tests each time with her thumb; everything has its precise place in her den. She never lights a fire, for it would be visible for miles around.

On two occasions, she went as far as the village, not the one closest to the fort – that would have been unwise – but the one on the far side of the hills, three days away on foot. She bought the couscous flour, the dates and the mutton fat from the elderly grocer, who looked at her with curiosity and ogled her legs, which were being nuzzled by the restless goats. For an exorbitant price – 'I'm not running a hotel,' he grumbled – she persuaded him to give her a bowlful of the lamb and chilli stew that was bubbling on his stove. Then she quickly left the village, in the opposite direction to that she would take to return, and once the last of the local kids had given up following her, she turned off the path and found a refuge behind an outcrop of rocks. Filling her hands and her mouth, she devoured the still warm food, enjoying the feeling of the heat as it slipped down inside her and spread through her body. The pleasure that she refuses, her teeth gritted – when like a hostile stranger it threatens those most intimate parts of her – with the soldier. The priceless pleasure – stored in the back of her mind, preserved in the very depths of her body, and almost obliterated, much to her despair each night – of the memory of Elijah's face. Of the body of Elijah, her man.

Twice, in two years. And each time she felt this pain within her as she trod the very long path which, once it had wound its way out of sight of the village, took her back towards the fort, to the man who was dying alive – should she believe that he was still alive? – who was dying an endless death down there. The man whom she kept alive so ferociously, and with such difficulty, deep within her being.

She waits. Down below, the fort with its scattering of lights seems to be suspended in a void, floating in the dark velvet of the night. She knows that the soldier, should he come tonight – and he will certainly come, for it's a day when he is off duty – will not wait for the moon to rise. He will come, clumsy and crude, and young and affectionate too – and rough – the thick cloth of his uniform, which he will very quickly remove, stinking of the barracks. And she will avert her gaze so as not to see the dark, smooth skin of his chest and the silvery glow of the moon on his rounded shoulder. For the hundredth time he will repeat his name:

'Ahmed! Why do you never call me Ahmed? My name is Ahmed!' And for the hundredth time she will shake her head and say nothing, and in her inner self, for her own sake, she will only call him the soldier. For she knows that she will kill him soon. But not before . . .

That's him, down below, that tiny figure stealing across the main square of the fort, zigzagging between the wells, possibly skirting the one in which Elijah waits, and waits. The man disappears into the shadow of the clay wall, but she recognises him again as he cautiously opens the wooden gate, which he quickly closes again. And she prepares herself. In a few minutes he will be there.

Ahmed stops for a moment among the labyrinth of rocks that he knows so well by now. He rearranges his jacket and runs a hand through his black, swept-back hair. He has been meeting her for over a year now, over a year since the morning when, having left the precincts of the fort after his night on duty, smoking a cigarette and breathing in the still-chill morning air, he noticed the goat high up among the rocks, in pursuit of the rare tufts of dried grass and lichen that grow among the stones. He returned to his sentry-post, a few yards further back, to search for his rifle. The goat was still there; it was looking in his direction. He took aim. In his sights, obscuring the goat for a second, he saw a white shape go past. He lowered his rifle; she had already disappeared behind the rock, but he had seen her. A woman, he muttered to himself in disbelief, it was a woman! And the word itself seemed just as unreal to him as the apparition.

She was waiting for him, squatting behind a rock, and when she looked at him fearlessly with her very black, very large eyes, he knew immediately that she had done this on purpose, that she intended this meeting. He had heard tell of whores who loitered around military camps, but he had never seen any near this isolated fort, far removed from the closest town worthy of that name, and which housed about ten soldiers, or rather gaolers, half of whom were released every two years. He himself was counting the days, barely two months, that remained for him to die of boredom in this forgotten corner of the world.

Not entirely forgotten, it was true. The

fort was linked by radio to military headquarters, and a briefing had to be submitted each week. More often than not, this amounted to a laconic 'Nothing to report'. Very occasionally, they requested that a soldier who was ill should be relieved. They also had to inform them about the deaths of prisoners. There were forty or so of them, and hardly a month went by without their having to haul out of its hole a corpse that was astonishingly light, with dull, staring eyes and a face shrouded in beard. It was the only moment – and it induced a vague sense of unease – when the hastily dismissed notion crossed the soldiers' minds that they belonged to the same species. It was strictly forbidden for them to communicate with the prisoners, or to respond at all to their prospective requests or petitions. In any case, these soon ceased, giving way to gloomy resignation. And the only contact that the soldiers had with them, apart from getting rid of their finally liberated bodies, consisted in once a day, as part of their morning duty, pushing around to each of the wells the cauldron of hot food, which the cook prepared in specially allocated premises, set apart from the kitchen, together with the barrel containing fresh water, and another one into which the excrement was poured, which would be emptied outside the camp, in the ditch that was downwind, so that as little of the foul smell as possible should reach the fort. They removed the heavy wooden lid, they changed the three cans in silence, and they clamped it shut again until the following day.

Sometimes, they tossed a stone at a prisoner who appeared not to move, and were satisfied by the faintest reaction that would prove he was still alive. Some soldiers, generally those who had recently arrived, were attracted by the easy opportunities for bullying. A gob of spit, a stone tossed pointlessly. On several occasions, Ahmed had seen them laughing as they urinated into a well, or upset the bucket of excrement over a prisoner. Such acts were not approved of by the others: not so much out of any humanitarian concern, but because they violated the required indifference. To humiliate a man was to acknowledge that he was still a human being, and in their confusion the soldiers sensed that they could not feel at ease in a place like this if they treated those who survived beneath the ground as humans. The sergeant in charge of the fort, a taciturn fellow who, at his own request, had held the job here for over ten years, had even punished a young man who, in his merriment, had spilled a pail of excrement into the fresh water barrel. Without going into unnecessary details, he had ordered him to clean out the barrel, fill it again, and sentenced him to a month of doing the filthiest of all jobs; emptying out the buckets.

From time to time, it was announced on the radio that a detachment of military police was on the way. The sergeant checked that the guard was standing in the correct position at the main gate and waited for their arrival, which was announced by a cloud of dust on the horizon. He would then adjust, if need be, the appearance and the stance of the guard on duty, remind him how to present arms, and stand to attention himself to welcome them. Two or three jeeps entered at speed and stopped by the administrative building, so called because it contained, apart from the kitchen and the refectory, the sergeant's office and his bedroom. The second building was used exclusively as a barrack-room for the men.

The jeeps disgorged men with hard faces.

They often brought with them one or two new convicts, whom they hurled to the ground like sacks, and who were dragged away on the sergeant's orders to the vacant wells. Sometimes, they ordered a prisoner to be freed. The sergeant would go and search for the sheet of paper that indicated the positions of the wells and alongside each of them, scribbled out several times according to the number of deaths and new arrivals, the names of their occupants. Each time he prepared a fresh copy, which he handed to the police when they set off again.

'What's the point?' the lieutenant who commanded the police detachment had once asked in amazement.

'I don't know,' the sergeant had mumbled. 'If there happened to be a fire, or something . . . You wouldn't know who was in there any longer.'

'And so?'

'And . . . if you wanted to question one of them . . . How?'

'Precisely!' the lieutenant had said with a note of astonishment in his voice.

And he had carefully folded the sheet of paper before tucking it into his uniform pocket. Though he did not say anything about it, the sergeant reckoned that hitherto his paper had probably been casually tossed away at the first opportunity. He derived an inexplicable comfort from this incident.

Only once, as far as the sergeant could recall, had they taken a man away; most of the time they ordered a prisoner to be brought up so that they could interrogate him on the spot. They used the same two steel-hooked gaffs with which they extracted the corpses. So much the better if the prisoner still had enough strength to cling on to them, or if they hooked on to a piece of clothing that held fast all the way. But often they happened to cut into the flesh. The soldiers did not like that and grabbed hold of the body as soon as they could. The police, unmoved, ordered that it be dragged to the refectory, where they closed the doors behind them. Often, when they emerged again after half an hour, or an hour, rarely longer, the prisoner was dead. Occasionally, he was still alive and was thrown back into his hole, but it was clear that his corpse would have to be pulled out again the following day. And the refectory had to be cleaned after they had left.

Apart from these interventions by the police, prisoners died . . . Nobody really knew why, and nobody cared. Illness, cold, consumption . . . Or perhaps they made up their minds to die, and succeeded? Some of them did not last very long: those who bellowed the most during the first few days, or those who were in a poor state when they arrived. Others, on the contrary, survived for a very long time. Only the sergeant could have said how long they had been there, and he did not mention the matter to anyone, and did not allow himself to think about it. However, he knew that one of them, at least, had been rotting in his hole for more than twenty-five years. A thought had occurred to him in this regard that bothered him greatly: in order to survive so long, he told himself, such a man could not really care much about life! This paradox preoccupied him for a while. He did not know what to do with such a notion, one that had come to him by chance, had forced itself upon him in spite of his attempts to get rid of it, and which he dimly suspected pertained to him as well. One evening he had drowned it in alcohol, he being the only person in the fort to possess a supply.

3

SITTING CROSS-LEGGED ON THE RUG AT the entrance to her den, silent and still, Tamia waits for the soldier. She listens for the sound of the stones that roll away beneath his footsteps as he approaches, from afar, in the cold, clear night. In a moment his silhouette will loom up before her, obscuring the stars. In a moment, once again . . .

She had very soon disabused him, rejecting the banknotes that he had hesitantly held out to her. No, she was not a whore. Nor a goatherd, even if the creatures provided her with a pretext and helped her survive. She was there because – she had thought about this for a long time: if she wanted the soldier to help her, she must not say 'her man' – her brother was imprisoned in the fort. For the past two years.

First, it had been necessary to find out if he was actually there. She had obtained this information – and paid for it with the only money she had at her disposal, her body – from an employee of the military police office in the capital. She had done so at great peril. Having satisfied herself that she had this man under her thumb – he was married, and she met him at night in the office which he guarded – she had brazenly threatened to denounce him and their relationship. She knew that adultery brought greater risk to her than to him, but there was nothing else she could do. The man was frightened. He agreed to rummage through the registers; he found the proceedings of Elijah Al Mansouri's trial, and seized on the findings: he had been transferred to the prison at Achkent.

'Are you certain?'

'It's what's written there,' he said. 'Are you satisfied?'

He switched off the light and came over to her, dragged her impatiently towards the box-room, where he had placed a mattress on the floor. She lay down once more, for the last time. When he penetrated her, she took hold of the knife she had slipped under the mattress when she laid down her coat, as she did every time. This same knife that was now concealed beneath her tunic, behind her. With a steady motion, repeated a thousand times over in her mind, she plunged it into the man's side, under his ribs, aiming towards his heart, which it pierced with ease. She saw more astonishment than pain in his suddenly wide eyes, and she extricated herself as soon as he collapsed on top of her. She withdrew the knife, wiped it on the discarded body, dressed without undue haste, and left by the usual exit without anyone noticing her.

Far away from the office, on the outskirts of the town where her sister lived, she asked questions. Achkent? No one knew of it. Or wanted to know of it. Occasionally, it seemed to her that this name aroused fear among certain people. It was an old man who eventually told her. Over there, he said with a wave towards the south. At the edge of the desert. His nephew had spent the first four years of his military service there. He had returned changed and peculiar, and he scarcely ever spoke. It was a bad place.

She bought a map and worked out the route, some 250 kilometres to the last town on the slopes of the mountains, on the verge of the desert. It took her two days to reach it, travelling in old buses that rattled from village to village. On arrival, she spent what remained of her money – apart from a small amount she kept for herself, and especially the bundle of notes she had carefully tucked into her belt and which, she did not want to doubt, would be used for her escape with Elijah – on buying a coat and some woven woollen rugs rolled up with objects she thought would be needed, and, from an old woman whom she met just after she had left the town, three goats, which were reluctant at first and had to be tethered, but which soon grew accustomed to her and could be released once they reached the hills. She walked slowly, for she had to allow the animals time to graze on the rocky slopes. She followed them as much as she drove them, for they had an unerring instinct for finding water, springs or pools in the hollow of rocks in which they quenched their thirst; the grass was too dry for them to survive without it.

In this way she took almost a month before she arrived at the precincts of the fort one evening, its lights twinkling below. The man she had come to find was there, so near that in a few strides she could have joined him. She suddenly felt very weary. Reaching this place had been her one aim, she had put all her energy into achieving it, and now, cast into a kind of stupor, her mind refused to contemplate further. This condition lasted all night, as she hovered between life and death rather than sleep and wakefulness. It was the horror which revived her. Which overwhelmed her, initially, when the following morning, observing the comings and goings in the fort, she was obliged to face the facts: it was in those wells, which the soldiers opened and then closed one byone, that the prisoners were being kept. That Elijah had been buried alive, for two years, inside one of them. That every morning the lid of his coffin was slammed over his head. She could not think of it dispassionately: she was Elijah, she was dying of anguish and solitude with him, she was his contorted body, his beloved, tortured, forgotten body. A frenzy of hatred rose up inside her that might have killed her, unable as she was to banish from her mind what she had seen, what she had felt. When, at last, it subsided, she knew that she would be able to kill again. She got to her feet once more.

She set up her makeshift camp in a sort of small cave between two rocks and concealed the entrance with a rug. She laid out the other rug on the ground and arranged the few things she needed. An hour's walk away there was a spring where she could replenish her supply of water. She did not have to worry about the goats venturing near the fort, for the grass they sought only grew in the hills, on the opposite side. Throughout long weeks she watched the movements of the soldiers closely, until she knew their routine exactly.

She had no plan, no precise scheme, she thought only of this paramount requirement: to know where Elijah was. And for that, she had to have an accomplice within the fort. She soon spotted a young soldier who seemed a little different from the others, who often left the fort, after his morning watch, or in the evening before nightfall, and who wandered about outside, daydreaming, smoking a cigarette and looking at the desert, while the others played noisy games of cards in the barracks. One morning, she made sure he noticed her.

4

Ahmed squats in front of her, not touching her, gazing at her. He is always amazed that in this darkness in which he can barely see her face, her eyes should be even blacker than the night. He knows what she expects of him.

'Tomorrow,' he says, 'the sergeant is going into town because we've run out of salt. I'll be on duty in the office, manning the radio. Perhaps I'll be able to find the sheet . . .'

'Perhaps?'

'I don't know . . . Perhaps it's locked in a drawer.'

'You must find out . . . Can you remember? Elijah Al Mansouri. Find him.'

'I'll try,' he says.

He stretches out his hand and touches her shoulder. A rounded shoulder, and very soft to the touch. She is the first woman he has known. She knew at once, because of his clumsiness and his haste the first time. She was surprised to find this touching, to experience a kind of fleeting tenderness which she immediately resisted. But she helped him.

She is the first woman. There had been his sisters, who were older than him, who played with him, and he remembered the softness of their hands. There had been his mother, and especially the smell of his mother, in which he would have liked to bury himself. All this is present again in this woman, in this woman's body. He still hesitates whenever he touches her, and each time it's a miracle that he has no right to be granted. It's not done without reluctance, he's only too well aware: that quick retraction of her skin at the moment he is about to touch her, that ever so slight recoil without her making any movement. The thin layer of cold over her burning body. He doesn't dare squeeze her breasts; his hands tremble when they fondle them and seem to dissolve on contact with her hard, almost indifferent nipples. Almost.

She does not give herself; she consents, she permits. Faced with the childlike impatience of his excited young body, she turns her head to one side. She allows her legs to be parted by his, and his penis, which has doubled in size, frantically tries to burrow inside her. He senses that she is looking at him from far away, from high above, with a calm gaze, and each time, in the unquenchable storm that cannot be held back any longer, when the entire life accumulated in his loins shoots out of him like a bolt of lightning, he feels frightened and ashamed.

But when, exhausted, he collapses on top of her with nothing but a swooning gasp and she puts her hand on his head to soothe him, he feels he is forgiven.

He does not know that in the immense and silent night that revolves above them, her open eyes are as hard and distant as the stars. Or that this hand, which she eventually removes from the hair she had been running through her fingers, will be placed beneath her white tunic and will make sure that the knife, whose hour has not yet come, is really there.

The moon has arisen. The still stones stand watch, and the desert grows cold. She extricates herself and wraps the rug around her.

'Tomorrow, will you do it?'

Yes, he says, tomorrow he will do it.

5

THAT NIGHT, ANDRÈS, THE MAN WHO IS determined to remain the man Andrès, stays awake. As a last resource, the biting cold is welcome. The cold has plenty of time to kill him. It plays with him. Before destroying him, waiting patiently for him to agree to surrender, it forces him for the time being to curl up tightly, piercing the contours of his huddled body with a sharp needle.

Get out. This notion which he had given up a long time ago – because it shattered on the hard stones of his prison, and because it would have killed him even more quickly, so scornful was he of its futility – had come back to him, quietly this time, desperately quietly.

Something occurred during the day that had aroused him. In that void in which nothing ever happened, something had happened. There had been the ritual changing of the cans, he had washed, he had drunk, eaten, and he had squatted down, back to the wall, without a thought in his head. It grew steadily hotter, a heavy stupor came over him, and his wide-open eyes were staring at the wall above the three cans. And they did not take in what they saw; they took an unbelievable time to take in what they saw: the rope and its hook were still there, hanging against the rock.

And even when he saw, he did not think. Not immediately. For a very long time still, he saw, looked, but did not think. He might not have bothered to start thinking! When he pondered it carefully – for now, at night, he could ponder – he might have spent the whole day looking at this rope hanging down in front of him without taking any notice of it. How had it come about – what was it that had prompted him? – that at a certain moment this vision should dawn on him, emerge, become clear in his mind, in the midst of the murky torpor that swept through him.

The rope!

It was the forgotten rope, with its brown iron hook, which was dangling in front of him.

He allows his thoughts to crystallise and arrange themselves. Probably because his mind has been unaccustomed for so long to thinking and has not needed to exert itself about anything other than the dreary passing of day, of night, the cans, the heat and the cold; because he has been bogged down in the mire of survival. But also because it seems to him that if he rushes them the thoughts will take fright and disappear, and the rope along with them, like a mirage when one draws too close to it.

Calm down: something is connecting him to the surface . . . to the world of the living . . . the rope . . . that hangs there . . . that is still there . . .

Will it remain there all day? Will they notice it before nightfall?

If he takes hold of it, if he tests his weight on it, will it drop uselessly to the bottom of the well, or will it hold fast?

And if it does drop? What will the soldiers do when they notice? He repels the notion in a fit of anger which galvanises him still more. What does it matter what they do? Is he so frightened, so reduced, that he can allow himself to yield to this fear like a cowering beast? Can he imagine the cries and the laughter of the soldiers when they pull the rope up out of his reach the next morning, while he plunges despondently back into an even darker night, into a living death to which he would have consented? He imagines it, he stands up and he bestirs himself.

He accepts and confronts the images: the rope is still there when night falls. It holds firm when he grasps it. Will he have sufficient strength to grip it? Sitting, squatting, standing up are already as much as he can manage . . . Yet he must. He now regrets giving up the exercises he had forced himself to do in the early months: bend his knees and stand up, lean against the wall and push back. He gradually stopped doing this. He betrayed himself, and in the worst way: unworthily. He did not realise; he does now.

Try to think of this: he has climbed up. He has succeeded in moving the wooden lid – how much does it weigh? And next? There's no point in imagining what happens next. He has only a very vague memory of the moment when, worn out by the days of cross-examination and by the journey on the floor of the jeep, they had thrown him to the ground before dragging him to this hole. The desert, without any doubt; he had felt it in the dry tremor of light, burning air. But whereabouts in the desert? There is no point in wondering about what happens next; he has to wait.

There is something he must do, however, which continues to hold him back. A first step. He gets up, takes hold of the rope and tests it as if he still doubted it was real. It is actually there; he can feel the roughness in the palm of his hand. He pulls gently, then with a little more force. Then he applies his whole weight.

The rope holds. He lets go of it, and sits down again opposite it.

He waits for nightfall.

6

The soldier, Ahmed, is sitting in the sergeant's office, opposite the silent radio set. He knows what he must do if it starts crackling. The sergeant had written down exactly what action he needs to take, and what words to use, on a sheet of paper which he has read several times. It is because he knows how to read that he was chosen. He looks at the radio suspiciously: without really knowing why, he is very frightened that it might ring. He is imagining the ruthless faces of the men from the police, and he doesn't know whether he will be able to speak.

He looks around him. The room is almost empty. On the desk at which he is seated there is an inkwell and a pen, and the sergeant's instructions. Nothing else. Alongside one wall there is a white wooden table on which stand the radio, black and disturbing with its dials and switches, and the microphone into which he may have to speak. Against another wall there is a metal cupboard that he has avoided looking at for a little while. He noticed, nevertheless, that it had neither lock nor chain. He wonders whether he will have the courage to open it. He thinks of Tamia, waiting up there on the hill. Whom he will meet before long. Who is waiting to know whether her brother is actually there. And if he is, in which well.

'When I've told you, if I can, what will you do?' he had asked her.

'I must know.'

'Yes. But then?'

She did not reply.

'Nobody has ever been able to get out of a well,' he said. 'Except . . .'

'Except as a corpse?'

'Yes. Or to be questioned by the police, then put back in the well. Or . . .'

'Or?'

'Once, during my time here, they took one away with them. We didn't see him again.'

'They took one away . . .'

'What are you thinking about?'

'About Elijah. Supposing it was him?'

He shook his head.

'No,' he said. 'I heard the name, when they asked us to pull him out. I no longer remember, but it wasn't that.'

'Are you sure? You say you no longer remember!'

'I'm sure it wasn't Elijah. I would remember. So? What are you going to do?'

'I don't know,' she said. 'Find a way . . .'

'To help him escape?'

'Perhaps . . .'

He is frightened. He gets up from his chair and goes to look out of the window. Two men are smoking as they chat in front of the sentry-post. Four others are playing cards in the shade of the barracks. There is no one nearby. He looks at the cupboard and walks towards it. Grabs the handle, turns it. The door grates as it opens. He goes back to the window, looks out again, then returns to the cupboard. There's not much on the metal shelves. A few registers, several books, some military manuals.

A sheet of paper is sticking out of a large black register. He opens the canvas cover. It's a diagram. The barracks, the forty wells, all numbered. And alongside each one of them, some names. Rarely just one; usually a column listing names, all of which have been deleted except the last.

He closes the register hastily, shuts the cupboard doors, and sits down again. His hands are shaking. He looks out of the window at the fort swathed in sunshine, where all is quiet. The four soldiers over there are carrying on with their game of cards. At the sentry post, leaning against the doorway, the guard daydreams as he gazes out over the desert. The geometrical alignment of the wells in the main yard has the silent orderliness of cemeteries. The blackened, disused water tank with its two big iron wheels, parked alongside one of the wells, resembles some strange insect. The disorder in his mind gradually clears.

Fear. Irrational fear, of course. Reading these names, searching for that of Elijah Al Mansouri, going as far as he can with these forbidden acts he has already committed . . . Fear, yes, but not only fear. There are thoughts which up until now he has not really wanted to admit to, which he has held at bay, which he would still like to drive away – it would be easy – this vague and overwhelming fear would suffice. He would say to her: I couldn't do it, I wasn't able to find it, it was locked in a cupboard. That's what he would tell her . . .

She would know that it was untrue, that he had given up, or that he had not wanted to – she can sense these things. When he makes love to her, she knows exactly what he is thinking, she responds to his every thought, her body responds. He feels certain she knows everything about him. That's what he's unable to resist; it's what he loves, like a child.

This clear-headedness of hers: the sort that has nothing left to lose. Nothing but . . .

And for the first time, perhaps because he too has nothing more to lose, because it has only just begun to dawn on him, he asks himself: is Elijah really her brother?

Nothing is going through his mind as he might have expected. He is amazed that he is entertaining this notion, this germ of a notion, almost dispassionately. He confronts it. Other thoughts follow, sharp and painful.

If he tells her that Elijah is not here, will she leave, since there's nothing more to retain her? Nothing? Might he be able to join her, later? Would she be agreeable? Or would he, Ahmed, vanish for her like this fort that would no longer matter to her, her search having now become meaningless, like faded hope?

And if Elijah is here, and he tells her so, what will she do? What will she try to do? Could he help her? Help her to help him escape? Help her to leave with him? Help her to forsake him, Ahmed, who would be left to his memories in a desert that is even more deserted . . .

Pain, like blood that burns when it returns to a frozen limb. Pain, and certainty, without need for reasons. He gets up, looks out of the window once more, then walks over to the cupboard and opens it. Opens the black register and takes out the sheet of paper, which he places on the desk. And he begins his long perusal of the cohort of the dead and the living.

7

The rope is still there.

Up above, the circle of light, which has slowly grown dimmer and is less and less discernible, fades and vanishes, and Andrès is once more astonished not to be able to pinpoint with certainty the actual moment it disappeared. No more than he can when it appears in the morning. And he is smiling, yes, he is smiling! As if this preoccupation suddenly appears pointless to him, even though it has been the key to his existence until now. As if it were already no more than a memory. As if he were already far away from here. And he smiles again, thinking that he is like a child who smiles as he dreams.

He must wait; be certain that all are asleep in the fort. From time to time he sits up straight, stretches his legs and gets to his feet again, leans with his hands to the wall and pushes against it. He does not want to think that he may be too weak to climb up to the lid. He thinks of nothing else. Once more he tests the rope's resistance, as if he were afraid that it might have lost strength in the interim, as if he feared he might have been dreaming. Then he squats down again. And waits.

How long? How many hours? How can you count or dissect an hour in the black stillness?

He decides that he will raise himself up on his feet another ten times. That he will do the exercises that prevent stiffness ten more times. Then he will test himself, no, then he will climb up, he will get out. He does not know how long, how many minutes go by between his exercises, but it doesn't matter: his mind is made up.

That's eight now. And nine. He fights against his desire to speed up the counting; he forces himself to wait, until . . .

Ten! Fear. Not of what awaits him outside: the fear of realising that his arms are too weak even to lift himself out of this bit of earth . . . It suddenly occurs to him that he has not left this bit of earth, that he has been stuck there since . . .

Don't think any more! Grab the rope, with both hands, one above the other, at head height. Feel the fibre in your palms, squeeze it. Pull with your arms. Your feet leave the ground. Press them against the wall. Not too much, so as not to be too far away from it. Feel for the little crevices. Let go of the rope with that hand that is shaking and place it above the other one. Again. Again.

His feet loosen some pebbles, which make a dreadful noise when they fall on the cans. You should have thought of that and placed them against the opposite wall. It's too late. Climb.

This trembling in his hands spreads through his arms as far as his shoulders. Keep them bent, even if they seize up, otherwise they will be unable to grip. And he is astonished because all of a sudden the hand that has just released the rope has collided with the lid. He had vaguely thought about what he should do then, at what was probably the hardest part of his climb. He pushes with both his feet against the wall, clenches his hands around the rope, and, with his head, tries to raise and shift the heavy piece of wood. It does not budge. It will not budge.

He won't be able to attempt this a second time. He wedges his head more firmly under the lid, encounters one or two rough places that are painful, nails that jut out through the roughly assembled planks of wood, on which he gashes his forehead when he applies pressure; he relaxes his entire body in an effort that will be the death of him if . . . The lid shifts and slides away, allowing a splinter of night to grow gradually wider. He forces the lid open until he is able to gain a handhold, and then his body does the only thing that it can do; he levers one leg then another against the edge of the well, and his hand – how can the other one still hold him? – grasps the lid, and then, with the help of the other, raises it; his body clambers out and rolls away beneath the moonlight, and he lies there, motionless, with scarcely a breath passing through his gritted teeth . . . and his mouth opens to let the cold night air enter, and life returns to his burning lungs. In a moment he will open his eyes.

*

There's a massive dark shape, just above him. A sort of giant cask lying on its side, supported on two pitted wheels. The rope is attached to one of them, which is why it held fast. He musters the strength in his aching body, wipes away the blood that flows from his forehead and prevents him seeing. Before getting to his feet, he turns back to the well, grasps the edges of the lid in both hands, and before replacing it over the hole, looks down inside. Total blackness. He doesn't think: I'm out! With a surge of wild joy, he thinks: it's empty!

He raises himself up on one knee. He's surrounded by row upon row of wells. A gasp of horror. Inside each one of them, like a worm, there is a man. Like him. A larval, silent, living creature, hidden from the world. A surge of hatred. May fire, torrents of flame, descend upon all of this, destroy it and reduce it to ashes which, after the blaze, will fall anew in the grey moonlight, and let it start with those dismal huts over there. And that other shack by the entrance, where a light shines.

Get away. In the opposite direction to that light, which indicates that someone is on guard over there. Get away on all fours to begin with, like a frightened animal, then start to run, stooping, astonished that these legs can carry him, zigzagging through the tombs towards the rear wall. Which he reaches. Which is too high for him to hope to clear without some support. But where, a few metres away to his left, he notices a wooden door.

The clear moonlight leaves a shadow, a narrow patch of shade, at the foot of the wall. He crawls over towards it. Towards the door, which he touches at last with his hand. Which he pushes. Which gives a few centimetres.

8

'You've been a long time,' she says. 'The moon has already risen.'

Ahmed squats down in front of her, further away than he normally does, too far away to touch her. She notices this straight away and doesn't question him further. There is silence between them, all around them.

'The moon rises earlier now,' he says eventually.

His hands are pressed to the ground. He would have wished that his gaze could pierce the darkness and take hold of her for ever; she can sense this and it makes her anxious. Sitting in front of her den, her legs folded beneath her and her chest held high, she doesn't move. She would like to read the expression in his eyes, as she always does so easily, and she is unable to do so. Not because it is too dark; that doesn't really matter. But because this evening those eyes are not entreating. They do not display the distraught weakness that normally arouses a slight contempt in her, and a vague affection too, easily repelled, which does not deter her from her goal. No. Those eyes are insistent. And, like her, neither do they have anything left to lose, and that scares her. She relents.

'Well?' she asks.

He has not spoken yet, and she already knows he is about to utter the truth, but she would like to delay the moment and not hear it immediately. Something will be said, and whatever it is it will be something that may perhaps stop time in its tracks, or on the other hand set her on her implacable way. A great weakness threatens her.

'Well, I've found the sheet of paper. I've read the names.'

His tone is curt and dry. He can hear it himself, as if his voice were detached from him, hard and terse, and as painful for him to hear as it is for her. Tackle suffering with speed. He does not delay and the words tumble out, one after the other, mechanically, soullessly.

'I saw Elijah's name. It's crossed out. Elijah is dead. I don't know how long ago, no dates are given, but it's not even the last one; there are two others after him, which means it's a long time ago.'

Suddenly everything was eclipsed, the sky and the stars and the rocks and this man who had just stopped speaking. The night came flooding back and left in its place still more blackness, absolute blackness and nothing else, both within and around her. One thought alone in the silent howling of the world, those words as red as fire, as red as blood, calmly repeating themselves: Elijah is dead.

He was not there, while she was waiting, while she was hoping, while she was speaking to him. He was not there when she had started on her long quest. Her entire life, which had rallied during those long months when she believed she was drawing closer to him, her whole life vanished with him. She was no longer there either.

How much time flows by beneath the pitiless stars, beneath the pale-faced moon?

At last she recovers a little, just enough for a fragment of the world to exist once more, just enough to be aware of the man who stands still and silent before her. He notices; he reaches out his arm.

Tamia thinks he is going to touch her. Whether anyone, he or she, dies as a result scarcely matters. She reaches behind her for the tunic, searching for the knife.

But Ahmed has withdrawn his hand midway; the gesture seems to expose the things that divide them, the unhappiness between them. Her own unhappiness, as well as his, Ahmed's. Expose the woman whom he believed he had attained but who had always been far from him. He speaks, and his voice which a moment ago had dried up has recovered its texture, and its human sadness.

'Elijah wasn't your brother, was he?'

Tamia's hand remains suspended above her white tunic.

He continues: 'I knew. I think I've known it for a long time.'

Slowly, Tamia puts her hand back on his knee.

Silence, once more, but time has returned. The great sphere of the night and the stars surrounds them and sweeps them away.

Tamia has now stood up, and so has Ahmed, right in front of her.

'I'm leaving,' she says.

And she gently lays her hand, the one that had been searching for the knife, on Ahmed's cheek.

'I know.'

He shuts his eyes for a second, then turns his head away resignedly. He looks at her again, and there may have been a smile. Then he sets forth into the night, towards the fort.

9

Gently. A plank of wood is propped against the wall; it is normally used to secure the nearby gate, as is evident from the grooves here and there. But it has been removed and the gate left slightly ajar. Andrès is amazed and feels suspicious, as if it were a trap. He stops and listens, holding his breath, but nothing disturbs the night and the silence. Are they so sure that nothing survives, either outside or inside? So sure that this spark of life which he feels, stubbornly enduring inside his battered body, cannot exist? Inside him a man who fears he may be glimpsed like a glimmer in the night!

Push the gate gently, just enough to slip through it. Close it, gently. With all the strength it takes to control his movements!

He leans against the wall. He is outside. There is something of the fort that still adheres to him: the stench. It's very close to him, a heap of refuse, the camp's rubbish dump. The thinner, sharp air is further away, towards the dark hills nearby. That's where he must go. As far and as high as possible, before dawn breaks. Before the circle of light forms up there, surrounding the lid of the well, where there is no longer anyone to wonder at what moment it appeared.

Leave, with this body that aches from the slightest movement, these legs that barely support him. In particular, he must not go round in circles during the night, once out of sight of the fort. On the horizon, just above the desert, twinkles the Southern Cross, which his brother taught him to recognise so long ago. He knows that it will not alter its position at all during the night, before disappearing at dawn. He will chart his way by it, so as not to get lost. He will keep it firmly to his right, at right angles to his path, in order to travel east. Why to the east rather than elsewhere? He has no idea of where he is; he does not know whether there is a village or a town in this direction. Perhaps the hills, and then the mountains whose jagged crests he can see, black against the starry sky, extend endlessly, much further than he will ever be able to travel. But the east rises diagonally in the hills, that is the only reason.

The rocks are very close. He reaches them as quickly as he can, and, sheltered by their shadows in the moonlight, avoiding the path of the gullies wherever possible without deviating too much, he moves further away, each precious step bringing pain.

Stop. Don't move. A stone rolled away in front of him. And another. He crouches down behind a rock, his hand selecting at random a long, sharp stone, which he clenches. There is still this noise, close at hand, and a sound of breathing. He gets ready to loosen his shoulder and his arm. He is no longer exhaling.

The goat's head, incongruous and comical, with the pointed beard of an old Chinaman, appears behind the rock and stares at him. He allows the air to escape from his lungs; it's enough to make one laugh! He holds out a hand to the goat, which steps backwards, but does not run away. And a second head appears, slightly tilted to one side, wearing a curious expression.

He would like to touch them. They are living creatures, which must be warm and gentle.

A voice, behind him.

'What are you doing . . .'

The soldier will not complete his sentence. Andrès' body – of its own accord, without him taking any decision, as he did a little while ago when leaving the well – uncoils like a spring, like a snake caught unaware, and the stone strikes the temple without the soldier even being able to raise his hand. And Andrès is this stone; he can see and feel it penetrating and thrusting into the skull.

The soldier is stretched out on the ground, his eyes staring at those of Andrès, his mouth opening as if he were about to speak, but no sound issues forth. He tries to move his arm but cannot manage to do so; there is a flicker of upward movement, but it slumps back again. The eyes, only the eyes still have life in them, but they are glazing over already. And they turn away from Andrès' face and stare into the beyond. Andrès follows their gaze, and . . . there, where the goats that have now fled first appeared, stands a woman. Tall, erect, motionless. A statue of a woman.

10

THE OLD WOMAN REMOVES THE RUG THAT hangs over the unframed window and rests her elbow on the window-ledge. It's her usual position, her observation post, from which there is never anything to see apart from the sweep of hills that cascade down, barren and chaotic, to the valley, which is not visible from here. It is only the immensity of the sky, from which the sun will shortly disappear in a wash of mauve that extends to the horizon, that allows one to imagine the desert stretching out endlessly over there. The old woman has never ventured down to the plain, but when she goes to the village, four hours' walk away on her spindly yet sturdy old legs, which she does without fail each full moon, she stops for a while before reaching the first houses, at the very point where, from the bend in the path, beyond the last hills, the great black expanse of the *reg* suddenly appears in the distance, and beyond that again, the ocean of dunes. She stops, and she looks. That slender patch over there, where the sand becomes sky and where the hot air quivers as they merge, that is where the world ends.

She then thinks about the end of her life, drawing closer with every journey, and she sighs before setting off again. It is not a sigh of regret. Nor of solace. It is a sigh, that is all. She often sighs.

Up until last autumn, there had been the donkey. But he was very old. On the previous journey, before the cold weather, he had refused to leave the paddock. When she returned, she already knew that she would find him dead. It is a worry, especially as far as bringing back wood before the coming winter is concerned.

When she climbs the path back to her home, on the return leg, setting her bags down occasionally to gather her strength, she also sighs at the point at which she spots her house. Up there, in the hollow of the mountain, you have to know how to distinguish those sparse ruins that are the exact colour of the rocks among which they nestle, and that are only recognisable because of their geometry, the vertical and horizontal outlines which the indefatigable winter winds erode a little more each year. Like her, you have to know of their existence beforehand. And you need the keen, clear sight – like hers, which has never faltered – of a bird of prey.

Her house is the only one among the ten or so that make up the hamlet to still vaguely resemble a house. The others have crumbled or have been ravaged and worn away, mainly by the wind and the weather. Some of them no longer exist except in her memory. She is alone here; one by one everyone else has left, alive or dead. She was alone. Until they came. She sighs.

Leaning at her window, she can see the goats, calmly searching crevices still for a few last tufts of grass, and drawing closer to the house as evening approaches. Soon they will have to be milked, before night falls. The woman will help her; she is good at that. There are eight goats now, together with the three they gave her. There is also the little black billy goat she swapped in the village for a female in the early spring, the little billy goat that jumps like a demon from rock to rock. When does he have time to graze, and will he be serving them in the autumn?

She also sees the thin column of smoke, rising vertically in the still air, above the ruined house where the woman has just lit a fire. It is for that man, the old woman reckons, whom she looks after so attentively. She will light her own fire later. It is a very long time since she has had a man to keep warm. She has lost count of how many years. It was well before the son, and later the daughter, left. The son, to become a soldier. And the daughter, for the town, a long way away, as did the other young people from the village.

God willing, she may possibly see her son again, once more. After his military service he left to go and work in a country that she could not imagine, even when he spoke to her about it. He found a wife, and he has children, two of them, he told her the last time he came. Perhaps three now. He said he would bring them to see her one day, with his wife, but she does not believe him. Or else it will be too late. He used to come back punctually every two years at the beginning of winter. He brings her a little money and a few gifts. It was he who gave her the shawl that she wraps around her shoulders. He stays for a few days, sometimes a week, and he does the odd job – it is thanks to him that her house is less dilapidated than the others – and he leaves. He came before the previous winter set in. There is a long time to wait.

She never saw her daughter again. She doesn't know how she manages to live, or even whether she is still alive; she tries not to think about it.

The darkness falls very quickly and it slips suddenly into the gullies, constantly altering and reshaping the appearance of the mountains. The smoke is blue now. The man must be feeling better; she saw him today, in the distance, leaning on the woman's shoulder, and he seemed less emaciated and sturdier on his legs.

She gets to her feet, goes to fetch the jar, and stands on her doorstep. It is time to do the milking. She walks down to the winter pasture where the goats usually gather. The woman joins her, very erect in her bearing, and she also carries a jar on her shoulder; her long black hair, tied simply by a ribbon, cascades down her back. A good-looking woman, young, strong and resilient.

They sit down side by side on the worn stone bench, at the entrance to what was once a house and is now nothing but a shelter that has almost collapsed. Each of them has her own place, always the same one. The goats crowd around them, making short, shrill bleats. The milk reverberates in the jars to the rhythm of their hands and a warm smell envelops them, that of the goats, which is strong and pungent, and the much sweeter one of the milk. A little way away, the small black billy-goat is growing restless.

Occasionally, they exchange a few brief words. They speak the same tongue, but do not always understand one another. The words the old woman uses are often strangely distorted and guttural. Is it her age? Or the dialect spoken in these mountains? The younger woman sometimes looks up, gazes at her, and repeats a word she has not understood. The old woman always allows a little time to elapse, then says it again, accompanied by a wave of her hand and a few other words. The young woman nods when she has understood. Although they do not show it, both women enjoy these moments.

The same gesticulations, the same rhythms; the movements women make. When the milking is done and the goats have dispersed one by one into the dusk that has now fallen, they go back up again, walking carefully, watching where they put their feet, the jars on their shoulder held by one hand. They enter the old woman's house, and one after the other they pour the milk into the cauldron where it will be heated to make cheese. They don't pour all of it. Each of them keeps some in the jar, for the evening meal.

The old woman says, 'That's good.'

She does not say what she thinks every time, what comes back to her memory each time: 'That's good, my daughter!'

She turns round and gathers some wood to light her fire. The young woman sets off again, her jar much lighter, to the man who waits for her.

11

ANDRÈS LAYS ON A BIT MORE WOOD AND the dry bark of the cedar branch crackles; sparks spit and rise haphazardly before vanishing into the disintegrating chimney, then the flame spreads and makes the old walls dance. He smiles, because of the pleasure that fire always gives him and because of the sense of gratitude he feels towards it. The first men who had possessed it and learned to control it must have been like him, he thinks: worshippers of that joyful, friendly genius that drove away the cold and the dangers of the night. He does not remember having wished for or imagined a fire when he was in the well, nor even having dreamed of one. In any case, though it surprises him now, he did not really dream. Some thoughts, some confused images, perhaps, in a sleep which was never really sleep, more a prolonged stupor. Yesterday he dreamed. Léa was in his dream, a radiant Léa, whom he believed had risen from his memory; she walked in front of him, and her back, her neck, her hips had Tamia's supple, robust fullness. He followed her, without trying to catch up with her or touch her, but was simply happy to see her. He cannot recall the rest of the dream; they may have been approaching a cliff beyond which you could see the very calm sea, but he is not certain about this.

Tamia comes in, holding the jar in the hollow of her hip. Her face is beautiful, he thinks, beautiful and grave. He would like to discover her smile. He believes that he has the same strange feeling for this woman, this face, this body of a woman, as he does for fire.

He thinks of Tamia, who supports him, who almost carries him at times, during the long hours when they walk ever higher into the mountains, when his legs give way under him and when all he wants is to lie down and die. He thinks of the unbelievable strength of this woman, whom he has only once seen falter, when she pulled herself back from the edge of a chasm down which she might have fallen.

He had been lying on the ground, sapped of all strength, beside the soldier who was dying. The stone with which he had hit him and which he had thrust into his delicate temple was still in his hand. When she had come towards him, he had tried to strike out again, for everyone he encountered was an enemy, but she had placed her foot on his arm, and then her knee on his chest. A long knife gleamed unsteadily in her hand. Her gaze moved from the eyes of the soldier, who was already close to death, to Andrès, to his own face, which she glared at with an expression of burning hatred because he was not the man for whom she had been waiting for so long.

It was at that moment, in those few seconds, that he had noticed that she was wavering beside an abyss. She could have struck out; she could have killed herself; she could have died, even without the help of the knife. All this, as well as convulsions and torment, could be seen in these eyes that were blacker than the night, in this body that clamped him to the ground and which, towering above him, was outlined against the stars.

The soldier gave a last, tiny shudder, and his head lolled back. There was another period of silence, of total stillness, he saw the woman's eyes close for a second and then reopen again, and he knew that she had decided against death. She stood up and held out her hand – the knife had vanished – and she said, 'Come!'

They did not return; they did not cast a final glance at the soldier, who was left there in the night, but for a long while afterwards he could see him dwindling in size as they moved further away, and he knew that she saw him too.

She replaces the cauldron, which is kept constantly boiling, over the fire. Then she pours a little of the still warm milk into a hollow bowl that she passes to him with both hands, which he too takes in both hands, carefully, so as not to spill it. She watches him as he takes small sips, retaining the liquid in his mouth before swallowing. He likes the fragrant warmth of the milk on his tongue, on his palate, that sweetness that courses through him when he swallows it, and the thin layer that lingers and coats his mouth. When he hands her back the half-empty bowl, she watches his hands that are shaking slightly – far less so, but a little none-theless – nods her head and closes her eyes as she drinks the rest of the milk. Each time he waits for this moment, the only one that allows him to study her face, and each time he is astonished by the huge blue expanse of her eyelids. He always averts his gaze before she opens her eyes again.

* THE INDIGO BLUE PEOPLE OF AFRICA

She pours the wheat flour into the bowl. She plunges a tumbler into the cauldron and carefully sprinkles the hot water over it. With the tips of her fingers – these are the focus of his rapt attention now, and she knows it – she lifts and kneads the grains, pressing out any large lumps. Then, while the flour is thickening, she goes to get the piece of dried meat which hangs from a beam, covered in a cloth, in the coolest part of the room, a corner that the sun, which floods in through the crumbling roof during the daytime, cannot reach. With the knife, she removes a few very thin slices which she places on a flat stone, by the fire.

'There's not much left,' he says. 'Tomorrow

I'll set some traps. There are plenty of partridges, I've seen them.'

She looks at him.

'I know how to do it,' he continues. 'I'll need a piece of sheet.'

He points to the cloth that covers the meat.

'Half of that would be enough.'

She nods, takes a slice of meat, and with her teeth she gnaws off a bit and chews it slowly. He does the same. From time to time they take a little wheat flour in their fingers, which they place in their mouths, tossing back their heads so as not to lose anything. The night closes in around them, around the precarious patch of ground where the flickering flames still glow. The night is blue and limpid.

She gets up and goes to the door. She glances at the faint, fluctuating flame of the old woman's fire which filters through the darkness, almost imperceptibly at times. She removes the rug that conceals the entrance and comes to sit down again.

'We shall go down soon. The old woman and I. In three days' time.'

He looks up, says nothing.

'Not to the village. To the town. There's a big market.'

After a while, she adds: 'She must get a donkey. She'll need one this winter, for the wood.'

As if in answer to his unspoken question, she pulls back her sleeve and reveals the large gold bracelet that she wears on her forearm. It's the only jewellery he knows she possesses and he has occasionally caught a fleeting glimpse of it.

'I'll go with her.'

A little later, they stretch out on the bed of dry grass held together by a rug. They pull another rug over them, the thickest one. They don't touch one another. He can smell the warmth of her body, a few centimetres from his. Or perhaps he imagines it. He can hear her soft breathing. Another human being, a friendly body, beside him. He watches the fire slowly go out. A small flame is sometimes rekindled, flickers for a moment, and then disappears. The night keeps watch; he falls asleep.

12

Yes, she takes good care of him, the old woman reflects as she watches them skirt the shoulder of the hill each morning and disappear in the direction of the spring. He leans more lightly on her now. She knows what they are going to do because she climbed up above the village on one of the first days after their arrival, to a place from which you can survey the valley, and where, in summer as in winter, the water surges up into a crater at the foot of a large rock, which is surrounded by mosses and long grass that the sheep, for some reason, spurn. There they were, and at first she had thought they were making love when she saw the woman straddle the man, who was stretched out on a flat rock. But the man was lying on his stomach, naked, and the woman was running her hands over his shoulders and down the length of his back, and so she realised she was taking care of his body.

She has forgotten what a man's body is like. When her man died – when his breathing, which was growing ever fainter, ever shorter, finally stopped, no longer racking his emaciated chest which each of his ribs seemed to want to pierce, such was the effort, such the pain for so little air – any memories of pleasure deserted her for good. Only one thing has remained, a stubborn memory that is awoken each time she handles one of the everyday objects or tools that he once used: his dry, gnarled hands, and she can see quite clearly the tendons moving beneath the rough, mottled skin. But not his hands on her; no, that departed with him.

Andrès is lying down, naked, on the large rock near where the moss keeps the water cool. Tamia is pouring a little palm oil into her cupped hands. Her hands slide, gently to begin with, along one of the man's legs. Then they become more forceful, more urgent, as her hard fingers ply and thrust deeply over the course of the innermost muscles. She works on the ankle and the knee. Andrès recalls the pain these movements caused him in the early days.

It was she who decided on this morning ritual. First she washed him carefully. There was an unhealthy whiteness about Andrès' skin, which was close to rotting in places, and she worried that it might come away in her hands, which were smeared with the coarse soap she had borrowed from the old woman. He needed a little sunshine, but only a very little to begin with, in the morning, when the heat was not yet blazing. Every day she slightly prolonged the time she gave to restoring this pale and scrawny body to life. There is no place that her hands avoid; they roam freely over the man's belly and penis without the least hesitation, and Andrès feels no shame, no desire either, but instead a feeling of great wonder and joy that makes him close his eyes.

It was Andrès' hair, and especially his beard, that gave her most trouble. Beneath the close-cropped thatch, the skin was damaged and appeared to be decaying. The old woman had only some crude, ineffective scissors. It was

Tamia's knife, sharpened repeatedly on a flint, which gradually trimmed, thinned and cleared this greyish web until it disappeared. Andrès' hair is now beginning to grow again, black like his beard, which she shaves every day. They have been there for over two months; summer follows spring and the sun is up before them each morning, blazing down directly above the valley.

Then she fills the pitcher that she has brought and they go back to the village, and he can feel that his legs are stronger and his whole body restored by the air and the sunshine. Out of habit she makes a second journey, on behalf of the old woman, and from the doorway where he still lingers he watches her return, straight and supple in her gait, the pitcher held by one hand on her shoulder, and he is amazed that her head and her back can remain so proudly erect while her feet steady themselves on the stony path and her legs and hips sway beneath her tunic.

That day, he takes the knife and cuts out a patch from the material that protects the meat. He cuts out three thin strips which he rolls between his hands, then carefully plaits them, and rolls them again until he has made a sturdy, thin cord; he then tests its resistance and, in the evening, he leaves it for a long time in the smoke of the hearth.

'It's to take away the human smell,' he says in response to Tamia's silent, questioning look. 'Tomorrow, I'll go and lay some traps. Two, maybe three.'

So there are some things that he did not know he could still do with his hands, but they return of their own accord when the need arises. Very early the next day, before the sun has even fully risen, he sets off to lay the traps. He takes a little wheat flour with him in a goblet, and he refuses to allow Tamia to accompany him, saying that he will meet her at the spring.

'I'm not going far. They're just over there, I saw them yesterday,' he says as he leaves. 'They don't suspect a thing, they haven't been hunted for a long time. Later on, it will be more difficult.'

She watches as he walks away, assessing the steadiness of his slow footstep, until he vanishes behind the shoulder of the hill. She then goes back, and hears herself sighing like the old woman.

Soon, she will have to leave: a thought that she dismisses, that returns insistently. Where would she go, and why? Nobody was expecting her anywhere. Her sister, perhaps. Yasmine, with her sweetness that was always slightly worrying, who must sometimes think of her. She looked so like their mother. Hazy images, faded with time, so long ago. Two little girls cling to their mother, the men bring back the father's body, the women weep. Like a photograph that she is looking at, in which she features, she is the one who looks up questioningly at the mother's face, a face of stone. Her mother's desolate expression, a few years later, the same women weeping . . .

Yasmine, her children, her man, her warm house, Yasmine who is always attentive, who must think of her, surely. A faraway land.

Affection lurks like a threat that must be held at bay. Elijah had been dead for a long time when she yearned for his hands and her entire body desired him. You cannot trust passing time, a river that is unaware of the dreams of the men waving on its banks.

*

'Perhaps you came with him,' she had asked Andrès on the evening of the third day, when they were frantically climbing into the mountains. 'Perhaps you were brought there together, don't you remember?'

'I don't know; I no longer remember. Yes, there was another man with me, I think. Yes, on the floor of the truck, I think. They had beaten me up, I couldn't see a thing.'

Then he asked, 'Tell me . . . what year . . . what year are we in? Now?'

She looked at him in disbelief. In horror. There was fear in her voice when she mentioned the year. He was silent for a long time, his expression pained, impenetrable; he was delving deep within himself, down the long, frozen tunnels of time.

'Well,' he said, 'well, no, I couldn't have been brought with him.'

Another pause.

'So is that . . . so long ago?'

She could have touched him then, put her hand on his cheek. She did not dare. Could not.

13

THAT WAS WHERE HE SAW THEM SWOOP down yesterday, a whole flock of them, their wings curved in a semicircle towards the sun. If they return, that's where they will scurry about for their food, in that long strip of dried grass at the foot of the small valley. He sets two traps, taking great care not to leave too much of his human smell in the grass. With a stone, he bangs the wooden sticks he has brought into the earth and tests their resilience. He fixes the cords to them and sets the noose slightly above the ground, resting on a mound of grass. The right height. And the right size: neither too narrow – they would not venture inside it – nor too wide – they would not be caught in it when they flew away. He is surprised that he can still remember the precise procedure in this way. He breathes in the dry smell of grass warmed by the sun and with it there comes back to him an image of Jan, the man who had taught him to hunt and to trap birds, rabbits, and even deer, on the sierra. The same smell, the same sun on his shoulders. Why are some memories so clear, so immediate, and so many others hazy?

Find Jan again, perhaps . . . Somewhere in the world, his cameras around his neck, searching for pictures. First of all, he has to leave this place; he must, he's strong enough now. And sufficient time has passed since his escape. Are you sure about that? Talk about it with her, this evening. She . . .

He goes back slowly. Without realising it, he has reacquired his hunting habits: he scans the ground and carefully examines the crevices beneath the rocks, in places where the looser earth might reveal traces of a trail or the entrance to a burrow. There are no rabbits; the area is too arid. Lower down perhaps, closer to the village, where the blue-green ring of tall cedars begins, but he can't risk going there.

A run that is barely visible, that almost disappears beneath the rock, a scratch on the ochre-coloured earth: a wild-fowl, maybe a marten. Squatting down, not moving, he examines this minute mark of life, and just as he is about to stand up he realises that without his being aware of it he had seen, a few centimetres from his head, a large lizard that blended in perfectly with the aspect and colour of the rock on which it was perched, and which was now glaring at him with a beady eye. Had it not been for the very faint tremor in its throat, which was slightly paler in colour, he would probably not have seen it. The eyes of man and lizard face to face, not moving. What lies behind its black, mineral pupil? Thoughts, such as I have? Or nothing but alarm and fear?

In a flash, without the slightest flicker of its thick feet with their long and slender claws giving him any warning, the lizard disappears. Andrès stands up; his still unsteady legs ache, especially his knees and his hips, but the pain eases and then disappears once he starts walking again.

*

The spring is slightly lower down; Tamia is already there. Standing naked in the little crater at the foot of the rock, she is washing, her back to him. Once again, and much more forcefully, he is aware of this extraordinary sense of power emanating from her body: from her back, which tapers up to her broad shoulders, widening to a dark cleft at the small of her dorsal region; from the curve of her hips beneath her very slender waist; from her high, strong buttocks, and from her stocky thighs. Standing in the water up to her knees, she springs from the earth; she is rooted to it. He had forgotten that sensation of strange weakness that comes over him in the presence of a woman's body.

Léa . . .

And when she bends down to rinse her hair, he glimpses her bush, black between her thighs. May she not turn round!

She takes one step out of the water, picks up her tunic and puts it on. The material slips down her body and catches on her hip; she releases it with a brusque movement of her hand. He comes closer; she turns round and looks at him. Her face is serene. Without having intended to do so, he smiles at her for the first time. A look of very faint surprise, as furtive as a breeze in her eyes. A sweetness, too.

'Tomorrow,' she says as he removes the coarse linen shirt and the faded cloth trousers that the old woman had given Tamia for him, on the first day, without saying a word, to replace the tattered shreds that had rotted on him. 'Tomorrow you will be on your own. We shall set off very early, the old woman and I. For the town. It's the day of the great market.'

He reaches out his hand and touches the gold bangle that encircles her forearm.

'Was it . . . Elijah?'

She nods, without looking at him.

It is his turn to step into the water and wash himself. She waits for him. He emerges again and stands on the flat stone, baring his body to the sunlight; it is still gaunt, but one can see that his skin and muscles are revitalised. She will not massage him any more; they both know this without it being necessary to talk about it.

From the doorway, he can see the partridges flying past in the meridian light and disappearing behind a hill up there. He looks forward to the evening with that slight thrill of the chase, that curbed impatience, which he had forgotten.

When she begins to lay the fire, he leaves to recover his traps. He comes across the goats on their way home and proffers his hand to the nose of the little billy goat, which evades him and challenges him with lowered head. About a hundred metres from the valley, he stops and looks at the strip of dried grass in the distance. A movement: a wing flaps and is still, it flaps again several times, then suddenly stops with exhaustion. His pace quickens; so does his breathing and his heartbeat. The bird is struggling, lying on its side, tied by one leg. He covers it with both his hands and quickly smothers it. The other trap was also successful, but the partridge – how did it happen? – is dead, throttled by the snare.

There is no longer any trace of the wheat flour, which he had sprinkled in a line in front of the traps. He unties the cords; tomorrow he will return and set them a little further away. He goes back down to the hamlet, a partridge in each hand. One is still warm, the other cold.

He hands them to Tamia, like an offering.

She takes them, inspects them, and nods her head. She places them on a stone, halfway up the wall, and says she will cook them the following day, in the evening, when she and the old woman return. And the donkey, if all goes well.

'I'll prepare them,' he says. 'There may be some others. How long does it take to go into town?'

'Four hours,' she says, 'or five. We'll have to leave very early.'

Later on, she goes to get ready for bed. Some flames are still flickering in the fireplace. Andrès is sitting on the doorstep. She can just recognise him in the frame of the doorway.

'At night, you talk in your sleep,' she says.

Then, after a while: 'Who is Léa? Your wife?'

He does not turn round. He does not answer. Not immediately. He gazes into the night. Then, as if he were addressing the night, he says, 'My wife . . . Yes, she was my wife.'

Later still, he slips beneath the rug, taking care not to wake her.

14

They are two women, who are walking at dawn along the dusty road that leads to the town. Dispersed along the way are other women – alone or with their man, sometimes seated on donkeys, their legs dangling from one side and beating the ribs of the animal in time to its steps – who are also going to market. It's the biggest one of the year, the old woman had said. The one where there are most animals.

Each of them is carrying a light bundle on her shoulder, which she holds in place, using exactly the same motion of the hand, changing position occasionally from one side to the other: Tamia has the dead donkey's packsaddle, a light, wooden construction that she had kept hanging from a beam, and the old woman has two empty baskets made of woven straw. They pass a small group of women who are taking a rest and whose chatter dies down as they draw near. Some of them greet the old woman, whom they know, and they look at Tamia with curiosity. Perhaps they think she is my daughter who has come to find me, thinks the old woman, and she is happy at the thought. The murmur of voices, occasionally a short burst of laughter, resumes as they move further away.

'There aren't many left from my day,' says the old woman. 'Fewer each time!'

It is the longest sentence she has spoken since they left. Tamia would like to ask her age, but doesn't dare. Neither does she know her name. Ever since their first meeting, whenever the need arises, she calls her by the one given to all elderly women, a name that can equally well signify grandmother or old woman, 'the ancient one'.

THE * ANCIENT ONE

'Peace be with you, grandmother.'

That was how she had greeted her the first day, when she had walked up to the hamlet which she had only noticed because of the thin wisps of grey smoke rising up into the blue evening air. She had left Andrès behind; he was lying exhausted and almost unconscious in a fold in the rocks. The old woman seemed to be waiting for her impassively at her doorway and had probably seen her coming a long way off.

'Peace be with you, my daughter.'

She had explained that she had a sick man with her, who was waiting for her a little lower down; could they spend the night, perhaps a few days, in the hamlet? The old woman had listened in silence, then she had pointed to the least decayed of the ruins, the one where they have been staying now for over two months.

When she had gone back to look for Andrès, she had not found him where she had left him. Twenty metres away, on his knees, mumbling incomprehensible words, he was still trying to escape, on his own. Later, he will tell her that he thought she had deserted him. She had had to drag him, almost carry him, as far as the hamlet. The old woman had brought an armful of dried grass, which she placed in the most protected corner of the ruin, then she had come to meet him and to help him over the last few metres.

They had lain Andrès down and the old woman had gazed at this prone man, his eyes closed, sparsely clad in tattered rags. She had set off again, returning with some wood and a pitcher of water, and set off once more, returning again with a rug as well as a shirt and some trousers that had belonged to her man. Then, without a word, she had left them.

Tamia looks at her out of the corner of her eye as they proceed along the side of the road. She does not walk quickly, but she has not stopped once since they left. Tamia wonders whether she herself will be like this, later, much later on: an old woman with thin, slightly bandy legs, making her weary way, eyes lowered to the ground, perhaps lost in her memories. She sees the rugged profile, the lines on her face, the sharp hooked nose, the long years of toil and hardship that are etched on her grey skin. She wonders whether she, too, has known any happiness or pleasure; she must surely have done, she thinks, but then why should her body manifest only suffering? Will she, too, have time to become like this, to grow smaller and harder?

*

Nearing the town, outside the first houses, men are sitting on benches by the doorways in groups of three or four, drinking coffee and smoking, watching in silence as the women walk past. The first stalls appear, here and there along the road. Fabrics, kitchenware, increasing amounts of fruit and vegetables that have come from the palm groves. The old woman points to an alley leading away from the centre. That's where the livestock market is, she says.

'But what about this?' asks Tamia, lifting her sleeve and displaying her bracelet.

'Afterwards,' says the old woman. 'First we must find out the price of a donkey.'

Tamia believes she is right. Supposing she, herself, had been able to sell her bracelet and then realised that it was to no avail, that she could not buy the donkey. The old woman is wise, and Tamia is grateful to her.

The livestock market is a huge, sloping field, surrounded by walls. An entire section is reserved for donkeys, and you can also find mules and a few horses. The rest is shared among goats and sheep. The tethered animals look calm and sad. A mule kicks out at a stray dog, which runs away howling. Over there, those who are selling are exclusively men, sitting or squatting beside their animals, or else going to fetch water in cans from a spring at the bottom of the field. The women have laid down the packsaddle and the straw baskets at the foot of a tree, near the entrance; Tamia gives an occasional glance, but the old woman doesn't seem too bothered about them. She goes from one animal to another, sometimes feeling their legs or lifting their muzzles to inspect their teeth, skilfully avoiding being bitten. The men look at the old woman, then at Tamia, who is behind her, and they avert their gaze so as not to appear interested.

From time to time, the old woman enquires about a price. Some of them tell her straight away, in a loud voice; others hesitate. The old woman nods, and without discussing the matter goes to look at other animals. Finally, she returns to a group of four donkeys tended by an elderly man, feels one of them again, and for the first time turns to Tamia and looks at her questioningly. The animal is female and appears to be young and gentle. A cross of a darker grey runs very clearly along its back and its flanks. Tamia touches its very soft mouth with her fingertips and the donkey, which has enormous, sad, black eyes, allows herself to be stroked and does not try to bite.

'Yes,' says Tamia. 'That one.'

The old woman crouches down beside the man and mutters a few words. Tamia believes her to be offering a price that is far less than the one that was mentioned earlier. The man shakes his head and says nothing. Both of them remain silent and stare at the ground; the man plays with some pebbles. Tamia moves away a little; she will come back when she sees the old woman shake hands on the deal, then rise to her feet laboriously, but with an air of satisfaction.

'She's a good animal,' she says. 'And a good price. He's keeping her for us. We'll leave the packsaddle and the baskets with him meanwhile.'

Tamia goes back to collect them. The man sets them down behind him, looks at her for the first time and smiles. His very white and regular teeth, and his slightly weathered face, etched with deep furrows, make him appear amazingly young. As if a teenager had until that moment been hiding behind the mask of an elderly peasant. His eyes, too, are young and gay. She smiles back at him.

They set off again towards the centre of town. As they proceed, Tamia recognises the café where the bus that had originally brought her here had stopped. The last one. Later, she had continued her journey south on foot. That was in another life.

The narrow streets bustle with crowds of people streaming slowly among the stalls. Clusters of them stand in silence, gripped by the haggling which drags on endlessly; the vendors raise their eyes heavenwards, swearing that at that price they would be giving the goods away; the buyers pretend to lose interest, and return at the last moment; those who are watching make comments to one another and become animated as if they themselves were involved in the sale. Dogs wander about here and there among the legs of the passers-by, closely watched by the men selling meat, who drive them away with rags. Bicycles, and a moped towing a beaten-up trailer and belching out clouds of blue smoke, force a path among the crowd, clanking as they go; Tamia is amazed that they manage to get past without too many collisions, but the people put up with them and nonchalantly move aside. After the long silence of the mountains, she feels as if she were floating and being tossed about in an ocean of noise, bodies, smells and colours.

The old woman also seems to be a little confused. She doesn't know this part of the town very well, where the few remaining stalls have made way for shops, most of which give on to the street and have more sumptuous window displays. She points to a jeweller's shop, her eyebrows raised with a look of uncertainty. The vendor grabs hold of Tamia the moment she approaches, and in a torrent of words offers her necklaces, bracelets and rings. She shakes her head and succeeds in silencing him for a moment.

'I'd like to sell this,' she says, pulling up her sleeve.

The vendor immediately adopts a suspicious and disinterested look. He reaches out his hand. She hesitates for a second, then passes him the bracelet, which he examines and weighs in his palm. He beckons to the two women to follow him, goes into the shop and lays the jewellery on the pan of a weighing machine, finds the correct balance with his weights, mutters to himself, then does a quick calculation on paper. He shows the result to Tamia, then takes the paper away, rounds up the amount and hands it to her again. She has no idea of the bracelet's value, but knows that she must not accept so quickly; she remembers the old woman bargaining for the price of the donkey. She shakes her head and proffers her hand for the bracelet. The dealer gives it to her, but holds on to it at the last moment, pulling it away from her rather roughly just as she is clasping it in her fingers. Instantly, she feels a surge of rage well up inside her, but she shows none of this to the dealer and listens to him quibbling before eventually proposing a slightly higher price. She seems to hesitate, reaches out an unsteady hand in the direction of the bracelet, which he continues to refuse to give back to her, then, with a sudden movement, she snatches it from him. They leave to a torrent of insults.

Anxiously, they set off again. An old man catches up with them and discreetly leads them a little further away.

'That's not where you should go,' he says to the old woman. 'Over there,' he points to a sign on the corner of the street, 'they buy by weight, at the official rate, which is displayed, and they may pay more for the workmanship.'

He looks at the bracelet in Tamia's hand.

'It's a fine bracelet,' he says. 'Go on, they're not crooks.'

And, smiling at the old woman who looks at him suspiciously, he places his open hands over his chest in a gesture that is intended to show his impartiality.

'Neither am I!'

He smiles again, says goodbye and disappears. They look at one another, each of them feeling equally unresolved, before Tamia shrugs her shoulders and they make their way towards the shop.

There is no stall. You push open the big door to go in. The shop is huge, quiet and rather gloomy; the showcases along the walls and in the middle of the room display a mass of silverware, gold and precious stones that glitter beneath small lamps. They feel ill at ease and intimidated. A man behind the counter welcomes them. Tamia hands him the bracelet, which he examines at length and also weighs. He suggests a figure, much higher than the previous one.

'And what about the workmanship?'

The man smiles.

'I've taken that into account,' he says. 'It's a fine piece.'

He summons a woman who is arranging a window at the far end of the shop.

'How much?' he asks.

The woman also weighs the bracelet, considers it and names a figure, slightly lower than the one mentioned by the man.

'You see?' he says with a smile as he returns the bracelet to Tamia, who is watching the old woman.

She in turn hesitates, then nods in agreement.

'Very well,' says Tamia.

And as she watches the dealer take away the bracelet and put it in a drawer, and hears herself saying 'Very well!', she feels for the first time the sorrow that she has been stifling ever since she made the decision to sell it. A wrench – yet another, it sometimes seems to her – in the gradual severing of skin from flesh, of muscles from bone, the threatened interdependence of her limbs, this warning of collapse in her body, hitherto so compact, that had begun with the words of the soldier Ahmed, the dead soldier Ahmed, and remained with her throughout her flight. She gesticulates; a movement that stems from her belly, a movement she cannot contain; she stretches out her hand towards the drawer. The dealer gives her a friendly look, raises his eyebrows and makes as if to open the drawer. Tamia withdraws her hand.

'No,' she says. 'Very well.'

As they walk along the crowded streets towards the livestock enclosure, the old woman silent beside her, she wonders what she is fleeing from. In Andrès' case he knows what he is fleeing. But what is it that she wants to escape from in this way? Since she has nothing left, anywhere, what is it she still fears losing? For the first time, she thinks she might remain with the old woman, in the deserted hamlet. Waiting, like her.

The sun is at its highest when they make their way along the road once more. The old woman is holding the donkey, which is exceptionally docile, by the bridle. Tamia walks behind. She is amazed and touched by the delicate smallness of its hooves, which are placed one behind the other as if the animal were walking along a very narrow path. The straw baskets that hang from the saddle, barely filled with a few purchases – a rug, some oil, some flour and sugar, a bar of soap, some green vegetables that protrude – beat gently against its sides to the rhythm of its dancing feet. Two women and a peaceful donkey, on a dusty road, empty at this time of day, which rises steadily among the foothills towards the village. Three hours beneath the pitiless sun to get there, then the ascent up to the hamlet will be more rugged, a further two hours. They will be there by evening.

There, where Andrès awaits them. Who will have lit the fire to welcome them. Cooked the partridges, and may perhaps have caught some more. He really must be on his way again, try to flee the country. She thinks once more of the temptation that came to her just now: leave him to go on his own, and remain in the hamlet with the old woman. Their purchases, including the donkey, have left her with at least half the bracelet money; he will need some, she will give it to him. She can sense muddled, indecisive, conflicting thoughts rising up inside her. She lifts up her head. The donkey sways in front of her, the sun is beginning to set on the empty road, the shadows lengthen; they walk in silence as if in calm water. In the distance the old, rusty water tower, perched on its iron struts, indicates that the village is close.

15

'HAVE YOU SEEN ANY POLICE? ANY soldiers?' asks Andrès, without looking round.

He is sitting at the doorway, almost invisible in the darkness. He asks his question while continuing to gaze at the canopy of stars: their twinkling is barely detectable, but it is constant, eternal, a distant life that is immense and indifferent. He knows the stars and their galaxies, he knows the unfathomable depths of the sky. He is here, he, Andrès, at this most infinitesimal point in the dark mountains. It requires an effort, and it is strange, to return to this terrain, to think of a path, an aim, a future. It is necessary, and ridiculous too.

She is already in bed. The habit is soon

established: she falls asleep before him, he comes and lies down later. From her shaded corner she says, 'No. I saw nothing.'

'At the bus-stop?'

She shakes her head as if he were able to see her.

'No, nothing either. But the bus wasn't there.'

'Tell me again what the names of the towns were, when you came.'

He has asked this question several times already. As if he were struggling to carve the names in his memory, as if these towns, only two of them, very quickly lost their reality and he needed to reassure himself of their existence by pronouncing their names. And each time, she herself has to make an effort to recall them. She mentions the two names; he repeats them.

'I shall leave soon.'

He says 'I'. It has also occurred to him that she would stay here. Or would leave too, but later on. He has often thought about this. On her own, she is free, she has nothing to fear. With him, if they are stopped, she is his accomplice. The memory of the well . . . Are there women down there too? It is inconceivable.

Yes, on her own . . . On her own with her dead man.

And Léa? Leave the country, if he can, then let her know . . . Why do these thoughts seem to be so unrealistic? Why do they lack any substance and constantly evaporate in the darkness of the future, if there is one?

The only time that seems real is here, in the encircling stillness. Indifferent, like the stars.

Long minutes elapse, hours perhaps, could any night watchman say? The Southern Cross has risen, over there, just above the horizon. He had not realised he was expecting it.

He stands up. Turns towards the darkness where she sleeps, an indistinct shape beneath the rug. Lies down with care, in his usual place, making sure he does not touch her.

He is there, lying on his back, his eyes still open in the darkness, listening to her almost inaudible breathing, endeavouring, as he always does, to feel her warmth, close by his left side.

And all of a sudden, life and this world are turned upside down, something that is at once surprising and expected, abrupt and engraved in time. Tamia has grabbed his hand, pulls it to her and places it on her belly. Places it flat on her stomach, which he discovers is naked, and soft, and warm. She covers it with her own hand. This has just happened, and time no longer stands still. Fear is impotent against the storm, against the triumphant surge of desire.

'I will come with you,' she says, very softly.

It is a lengthy crossing, with a deep and powerful ground swell that nothing can halt, currents that are broad and low. A gentle discovery of bodies forgotten, revisited, yielded up, offered. Beaches of soft sand, the wonderment of skin, the cool of meadows, the velvet of flowing seaweed. A force swept along to the brink of violence, sought after, welcomed, loved, still needed.

A moaning, and the whisper of the wind, in their conjoined mouths. Which soothes. Which subsides. Which grows fainter and murmurs again.

They lie side by side. The woman's head on the man's shoulder. The woman's thigh on the man's, touching his soft penis, entrusting the warmth of her genitals to him. She gazes at the embers still glowing in the hearth. He watches their reflections in her eyes. Time slips by in tranquillity.

Tomorrow they will speak to the old woman. They will tell her that they are going to leave. That later, much later perhaps, they will come back to see her. They will restore her to her solitude, waiting for death. They will go away. Soon.

With his free hand he pulls the rug over them. They fall asleep, without parting. The stars keep vigil. The embers slowly fade.

16

THEY HAD SKIRTED ROUND THE VILLAGE, where he might have attracted attention, and rejoined the road, which she had taken with the old lady a few days earlier, lower down. It is still very early and the air has retained a little of the night's coolness, a slight touch which is already beginning to disperse. Cockerels call to one another beyond the hills and rouse echoes from the mountain.

As they walk, they feel and savour the harmony of their footsteps. They are two peasants on their way into town. On his shoulder, Andrès carries a rolled-up rug containing the few things they are taking with them. The knotted ends of the cords used for the partridges flap gently against his back and his chest to the rhythm of his footsteps. Tamia, beside him on his right, also carries on her shoulder the coat given to her by the old lady a short while ago, which she holds by the collar with one hand.

They had told her that they would leave the following day. A few words; there was nothing to explain. She was there, at her doorway, when they emerged into the newly dawning day. She came out to meet them, bearing her man's grey woollen coat which she wanted to give to Andrès. He bowed to her and she kissed him on the forehead. Then she turned towards Tamia, rummaged beneath her clothing and handed her a small object neatly wrapped in a clean piece of white linen. She placed it in Tamia's hand and folded her fingers over the gift, thereby implying that she should not open it until later. Tamia looked at the brown gnarled hand touching her own, which was young and strong. The network of veins and the strings of her tendons, the long years of solitude and hardship in the dry, scrawny hand, laid on her own smooth, clear one, which a few hours earlier, in the blissful night, was stroking

Andrès' body. She took it and raised it to her lips, and the old woman also kissed her, on the forehead. Her kiss was so light and her lips so soft that Tamia scarcely felt them. And she feels them still.

They are walking. They encounter a man who comes from the town and is going to the village. The man is perched on a small donkey, his feet almost touching the ground. He suddenly appeared at a bend in the track, they could not avoid him. The man stares at them. They greet each other with a nod of the head. Tamia waits until he can no longer hear them, and says in a low voice, 'He's not as handsome as ours!'

And since Andrès is looking at her in surprise, she adds, 'The donkey!'

They laugh, they hold their heads high, they know they are young.

On the outskirts of the town, some women bustling about outside their houses glance at them with an air of apathy. An old man leaning on his stick watches them more attentively and gives them the morning greeting. Andrès responds with a brief word and a nod of the head.

Tamia hesitates for a moment. This was the narrow lane they took to go to the livestock market. That was where she had seen the café by the bus stop, when they had turned back towards the town centre. They walk on, and she notices the small square, a little way off at the end of a street, which she points out to Andrès. They feel as if their footsteps are becoming more cautious, as if determined not to yield to the anxiety which has just gripped them. If there are any police checks, this is the most likely place they would encounter them. Andrès has no identity papers to produce.

He has no fear of being recognised, for he has forgotten what he looks like, the way he looked before, before the long, endless night. All he is sure of is that he is very much an outsider. Yet they imprison a man without papers, and they question him. They want to know where he comes from, what he has been doing. Does a place or a country exist where you can be totally new, where no one bothers about you? Beyond the sea, if they ever get there, would it be possible?

And because he had imagined himself at a port, searching for a ship, with Tamia beside him, he reckons it is not merely fear of the police that causes him to slacken his pace. There is Léa, whom he constantly forgets, and who constantly comes back into his mind. She is probably in the city, which he is not sure he wants to go to, and yet he must.

He puts his hand on Tamia's arm, so that she stops before reaching the square. They must travel separately, he says. If there were to be a police check, they must not be found together. She will go to the café first, to find out about the time of the coach and buy her ticket if necessary. He will wait for her here, and he will then do the same. She agrees, hands him the coat she was carrying on her shoulder – they both realise that it is much too tight for him, but don't want to part with it – strokes his hand and sets off towards the square. He goes and squats by the foot of a tree, lays down the rug beside him, and watches her crossing the square.

Léa. Would he have thought more about her, would he even have wanted to find her again, if there had not been these few months, almost three of them, spent with Tamia? He only has a faint image of her now, and it's not very vivid. He used to feel guilty about it down the well, he remembers – to begin with at least – then she vanished. Why did her face, her body, fade like this? Why could he not cling on to them?

But if anything remained to brighten the nights and make them a little warmer, it was not her. It was the images that came back from childhood, the face of his mother, gentle and always a little sad. It was also the laughter shared with Jan, his wonderful elder brother who knew everything and who taught him to swim and to hunt. It was his friends who were activists, the secret meetings, the long, heated discussions and the pasting up of posters at night, and also, more dangerously, the activities they embarked upon with thumping hearts, when they knew they were risking their lives and felt intoxicated by their own audacity. That attack on the villa where the political police held, interrogated and tortured their prisoners, and where two of them had died without being able to free their comrades. And the grief and anger of the frantic questions they asked themselves the next day: should they risk lives like this? What were their true aims? How effective were they, and were they justified? Questions he continued asking himself, down the well. Questions that kept him awake for a time, before they became confused, before everything became blurred and confused.

And the sudden, baffling wave of arrests, with no time to escape, nor even to warn anyone, when almost the whole of their group was rounded up within two days. That too, above everything else, had kept him awake for ages, furious at not being able to understand the mistakes they had made. And then even that had dissolved into the darkness.

He watches Tamia emerge from the café. What is it that has rekindled these memories in this way and taken possession of his thoughts to such an extent that for a second he is amazed to find himself squatting in the shade of this tree, in this square, as if he were suddenly seeing himself with the eyes of this woman who is walking towards him?

Who squats beside him and leans gently on his shoulder. The coach will leave in two hours. A good thing; he will go directly to the capital. No need to change twice, as she had done when she came, badly informed perhaps. She has bought their two tickets; it is the owner of the café who sells them.

'I told you . . .'

'There were three policemen in the café,' she says. 'Drinking tea, chatting to one another, and not appearing to pay much attention to travellers. But it may not be like that when we leave . . .'

'And . . . if we are stopped?'

'We shall leave one another and travel separately. Here's your ticket. If they stop you, well, by the time they make their investigations, if they do, I shall be far away.'

He tells himself that she is right. He likes to feel her shoulder against his. If they stop me, he thinks, I shall kill, before being killed.

The coach pulls up outside the café. A couple of peasants get on immediately, the driver takes their tickets. The police have not left the café.

'Go, now,' says Tamia.

He squeezes the hand placed on his knee and gets to his feet.

'Take the coat,' she says again. 'I'll carry the rug.'

He is on his feet; he has thrown the coat over

his shoulder. He continues to look at her, at her eyes, especially her eyes. Then he crosses the square in the direction of the coach, without turning around.

17

Tamia is sitting at the back, with the rug over her knees. Over there, almost at the front, next to the gangway, the back of Andrès' neck – attached to his shoulders by two powerful strands of muscles – looks somewhat fragile beneath his hair, which she really should have cut better! This man with his badly trimmed hair, his shoulders, his male body. She is behind him, close up to him, her bare breasts caressing and pressing against his back, while her arms clasp his shoulders and her cheek rests against his neck. They are so near – a few metres apart – and yet so far from one another.

She does not know what is to become of them once they reach the big city. Andrès must evade the police and slip away to the border, to the sea, and leave the country. To go where? They have not really talked about this, probably because there are other, preliminary questions that still have to be answered. There is this woman, Léa, whose name he sometimes murmurs in the night. 'She *was* my wife,' he had said. In the heavy silence he maintains, behind his almost childlike expression – but which can be closed and gloomy too – when he looks round at her, she knows, she can sense that this woman is present, that she weighs down on them, that she is threatening them. At this precise moment, inside the head that is so close to her, and which is gazing straight ahead at the road, that head she longs to touch and stroke, cradle in her arms and press to her bosom, what thoughts, what future does he foresee?

The mountains have now given way to the great plains and, beneath the huge dome of the sky, the coach crawls along like some large, noisy insect. Ahead, a totally straight road that dwindles into the distance, into the blank horizon shimmering in the heat. Behind her, a chasm of dead years, of time that has stood still. What has become of Elijah, and even the memory of Elijah, which continues to lose its lustre? In this coach, rattling along as if it were suspended, motionless, on this endless road, she floats, a survivor, between a stagnant past and this unimaginable future where death also lurks. Andrès . . . Elijah . . . My name is Tamia . . .

He watches. The danger lies further ahead, over there at the end of the road, and he wishes he could put a face to it. In his imagination there are policemen, an attempt to escape, shots fired; he imagines the worst, wounds, pain. He closes his eyes; the images are clearer.

He must have fallen asleep: when he opens his eyes again, houses are passing by on either side of the coach as they enter the town. Long avenues that grow increasingly busy, workshops, a barracks, children playing, men at work, a life into which one must merge without being noticed. They are turning into a square where other coaches are parked. In large concrete letters on a grey building are the words 'Bus Station'. People are getting on to a coach; their own one pulls up behind it and comes to a halt with a great sigh of the brakes. On the pavement, two policemen walk by, smoking, and do not appear to be especially on the alert. The door of the coach opens with a hiss and people start to get out.

Tamia would leave first and he would follow her at a distance: that is what they had planned, but they had not imagined that he would be the first to get off the coach. On the pavement, he hesitates for a moment in confusion. It is dangerous to appear lost or to look like a foreigner, it attracts attention; fortunately, he can see that Tamia has left by the rear door and is already on her way. He settles the coat on his shoulder and walks past the policemen, the tension gnawing at his muscles probably doesn't show, and he presses on, a man walking in relaxed fashion, his coat slung casually over his shoulder, a man calmly returning home. So unconcerned are the policemen that it makes his fear seem ridiculous, and he could almost – he thinks with a smile – almost feel disappointed that everything is going so smoothly.

A very long street, then another. At the far end of the third one, Tamia is waiting for him. All is quiet. He comes up to her, she smiles at him, touches his arm lightly, and they set off side by side. Yasmine might put them up, Tamia had said. At least for a few days. Her husband is a decent man, a motor mechanic with his own garage adjoining their house. He is . . . he was Elijah's cousin. But he was never politically involved, they have never been troubled, it's a safe haven. In which to wait.

Wait for what?

'There! The blue house, on the corner.'

The house is white: it is the shutters, the window frames and the garden gate that are blue. Pink, orange and red bougainvillaea hang in clusters over the façade and the railings. Adjoining the house, a white concrete garage, its door wide open, cluttered with cars. A man is at work beneath a hoist.

'It's David,' Tamia says. 'My brother-in-law. Come along now!'

She drags him over to the house, rings the bell and, without waiting, opens the door. A bright hallway, a door from which steps a woman wiping her hands on her apron, who looks at them and suddenly stops still. She lets out a cry, as if of pain, as she clasps and embraces Tamia. She is a big, strong woman, and she weeps as she buries her face in her sister's hair. Andrès watches them from the doorstep.

18

Dusk falls over the town and casts a pink hue over the houses basking in their faint scent of jasmine and honeysuckle. The gardens are quiet, the colour of the bougainvillaea trees softly fades. In the town centre the bright lights have abruptly eclipsed what remains of the day already, but here, on the outskirts, in this neighbourhood of small, peaceful houses, it lingers on almost reluctantly. One can still feel its presence, even if the lamplights have spread a shadow over the wide-open windows, and the voices around the table have grown softer.

The two children are seated on either side of Tamia. Leila is ten years old; her huge, dark eyes are fixed on her aunt's face and she is lapping up every word she speaks. Tamia, aware of her gaze, smiles at her. 'You're beautiful, Leila,' she tells her, and she turns to Pierre, who is five and intent on what he is eating. She strokes his round head and Yasmine, sitting opposite them, says, 'They've grown, haven't they?'

Andrès is in conversation with David, but he often glances at the two women and the children. The men eat slowly: David pours the viscous, almost blue wine, and they drink at the same time, savouring it and chewing the grape in their mouths between tongue and palate. The talk is of mechanical things, of cars. This occasionally makes a curious impression on David, though he is careful not to let any hint of it show: Andrès knows about engines, he speaks like someone who has dismantled and put them together, that is quite clear. But he has some strange gaps in his knowledge: he has never heard of any of the recent models and he is unaware of the existence of certain technical innovations, which poses difficulties for David. David reckons he knows what conclusion to draw, which is that Andrès has probably been cut off from the world in recent years, that he may have been a fellow prisoner of Elijah's, since Tamia has brought him back with her. But he says nothing about this.

A short while ago, just after they had arrived, Tamia spoke briefly about Elijah. Yasmine had summoned David with cries of joy, and he had emerged from the garage, wiping his hands on a rag which he had discarded the moment he saw Tamia. He had hugged her at length, he had looked at Andrès and greeted him, and he had turned to Tamia with an expression of silent interrogation.

'Elijah is dead,' Tamia said.

She spoke softly, and her eyes were fixed on the ground between them.

'He had died. A long time ago. Shortly after his arrest.'

David said nothing. He did not ask whether she was sure, or how she had discovered this. He took her in his arms again and clasped her to him. All he murmured was, 'I knew. Even before you set off to go there, I knew.'

Yasmine and Tamia are sitting in the kitchen. Leila is standing, leaning against her mother. Her eyes never leave Tamia; she watches her as she talks. She reaches out shyly with her hand and feels the material of her aunt's tunic. Tamia smiles at her, strokes her hand, and continues talking. She says she has no idea what they will do in the next few days. Andrès must find a way of getting out of the country, but he must also go and see relatives who live in the town. She says 'relatives' without elaborating further. She does not know whether she will go away with him. Yasmine wants her daughter to go to her bedroom, she is not meant to hear all this and in any case it is time for bed, but Leila resists, she wants to stay up. It seems to her that Tamia has a special, slightly wild smell about her, that she is not like her mother, that her face is different, even though they do look a little like each other. Tamia's cheeks are hollow, her mouth is framed with two delicate furrows; Leila would like to have a face like that, later on. She gazes at her mother's face, and up at Tamia again, then a far-away look comes over her as she leans more heavily against Yasmine who, while continuing to speak, puts her arm around her daughter's slim waist.

She pauses, then, looking down, she says, 'It's not easy . . . David . . .'

'I know,' Tamia says. 'He's right. It's dangerous. A few days, a week . . . Not more.'

Yasmine looks up at her again.

'You see,' she says, 'there are the children . . .'

Tamia takes her hands in hers.

'Of course,' she says. 'Don't worry.'

Yasmine raises Tamia's hand to her lips and kisses it.

'I'm so happy that you're here!'

'I know,' Tamia says. 'I know very well.'

A very thin crescent moon watches over the houses; the cool night air enters through the half-open window, accompanied by the rasping sound of a cricket endlessly repeating the same thin, monotonous note. When the noise stops, the silence grows darker and deeper. Lying side by side on the sofa bed in the sitting room, Tamia and Andrès, eyes wide open, ask questions of the night. Tamia's fingers lie light and motionless on Andrès' arm.

'I have to know,' says Andrès to the silent night. 'And . . . so does she.'

Tamia's fingers have not moved; they are holding back time.

'They must have been keeping watch on her

since your escape,' she says eventually. 'I'll go and see her, if you want.'

A few metres away, that same night.

'She's your sister,' says David. 'Is she going to stay with us?'

'I don't know. I don't even think she knows yet.'

Yasmine turns towards him and takes him in her arms. She likes to feel the compact thickness of his shoulders. As she does every time, she takes hold of him like this, and her hands stop in surprise as they run along his back, which always strikes her as unbelievably broad and strong, and she thinks: you are mine. She never says this.

Little Pierre is the only one asleep. Leila can hear his gentle breathing, interrupted from time to time by a sigh from the bed at the far side of the room. She can feel her girl's body in her flimsy nightdress, and she dreams – her eyes too are wide open in the darkness – she dreams that she is Tamia. She doesn't really dare imagine that, like her, she has long legs and firm, proud breasts, but she can feel them in her dream.

*

'I have to show you something!'

Tamia switches on the light on the little table drawn up alongside the sofa bed. She gets up, naked, and goes and rummages among her clothes. She comes back with a small packet wrapped in a white cloth. She sits down on the bed and opens it. It is a bracelet, made of very light silver braiding, and it looks fragile. She puts it on her arm and shows it to him, a friendly, lovable little snake, coiled round her forearm, in love with the warmth of her skin. Andrès touches it with his fingertips.

'She's alone up there,' he says.

He pulls Tamia into bed, leans over to switch off the light, and then takes her in his arms. Beneath his caress, the cool touch of the silver is like a sign of complicity.

19

'Her name is Léa,' Andrès had said. 'Léa Montaldo.'

'Did she never use your name?'

He had shaken his head.

'Andrès . . . Do you realise that I don't know your name?'

'Aslegg,' he says. 'Andrès Aslegg. There's no reason for me not using it . . . it's just that I find it difficult to pronounce. Even to myself, for myself. Well, perhaps less so, now . . .'

From the pavement on the other side of the street, Tamia looks up at the three empty first-floor windows, with their projecting wrought-iron balconies. Just below them, on the ground floor, there is a laundry. Andrès had mentioned a café, but a good deal must have changed since he left. This is where he lived, with her, Léa, whose face she is unable to picture.

A woman emerges from the house with a package in her hand. Much too old to be Léa. She walks directly into the laundry. Tamia hesitates, then she also crosses the street and goes in too. The woman is cramming her clothes into a washing-machine; she casts a sharp glance at Tamia, then continues her task. The room is huge and clean, tiled in white, and swathed in glaring light from the two neon tubes. It is hot, a damp heat that smells of washing. A row of machines lines one wall, some of them in motion. A sort of self-sufficient life of its own, grey and colourless.

They are alone. Tamia goes to greet the woman, who looks up at her with hard, mistrustful and questioning eyes, without returning her salutation.

'I must have made a mistake,' says Tamia. 'I thought there was a café here.'

The old woman shuts the door of her machine and stands up with difficulty.

'There used to be one,' she says. 'You can't have been here for a long time!'

'Yes. A long time.'

The old woman gives a terse laugh. 'Everything has changed here. Except me!'

'I didn't come very often,' Tamia says. 'Two or three times. My sister had a friend, there, up above, Léa. Léa . . . Mondiego, I think.'

'Montaldo! She's not there any more. And her name's no longer Montaldo. Maidani, I think. Yes, that's it, Maidani. Hassan Maidani is the husband's name. She lives in the fashionable district now. Down there . . .'

She gives a casual wave. By the sea, she says, and she has a swimming-pool. One of her friends was a waitress at the wedding. It had to be seen to be believed! No, she doesn't know the address. Those new, rich peoples' houses, not far from the sea.

'Too bad,' says Tamia. 'And good for her. And thank you all the same.'

'Not at all. Go in peace.'

'Peace be with you too,' says Tamia.

She turns round before leaving.

'Was it a long time ago? When she left, I mean.'

'Hmm. Three years maybe . . . No, four, I know it'll be four this summer; it was my granddaughter's christening.'

'You've a granddaughter . . .'

'And a grandson, four days ago,' says the woman.

She gives a broad smile, and her eyes gleam. Tamia smiles back.

'You're lucky,' she says.

20

There is a whole page of Maidanis in the local telephone book. Twelve of them called Hassan. Look in the fashionable district, as the old woman had said, by the sea. Two addresses seem likely possibilities. She jots them down and leaves the post office. Down there, at the far end of the wide avenue lined with palm trees, is the port. The beach is alongside it, she knows it well, she used to go there once upon a time, with a group of girls. The boys kept their distance. Knowing laughter, jeering, waves and sunshine . . .

It's a dangerous, very steep beach. The great rollers come from far out at sea and break there unimpeded. Dunes strewn with esparto grass tower above. That's where the rich peoples' houses are built: enormous white villas, an entire neighbourhood that did not exist previously. Roads lined with palm trees, and long walls to protect the gardens where the sprinklers play.

The first address is surely not the correct one. It's a street very much set back, with small, older houses that do not overlook the sea, and this one looks more or less abandoned. Closed shutters, a little garden overrun with dry scrub. She would like to have a house like this; she imagines herself repainting it, opening the windows wide and working in the garden, but these are unexpected, fleeting, bitter-sweet thoughts. One day perhaps . . .

The other address: Allée des Hibiscus. A man mending a wall gestures with his hand: that way, further on. The roads close to the sea have complicated names, those of flowers that are often obscure: physalis, agapanthus, epheradus . . . Number 16, Allée des Hibiscus has a high wall, roughcast in ochre, too tall to be able to see over to the other side. A solid, wooden, studded door, with no sign of any name.

A car drives slowly past. Two men inside look at her as they go by. She keeps her head lowered and doesn't stop walking. She wonders whether they noticed her linger in front of the entrance. Private guards? Or the police keeping watch? The car disappears at the bend in the road. She continues to walk along this endless wall which dips down eventually in the direction of the sea. A narrow path, separating these grounds from the adjoining property, runs down to the beach. It is covered in sand and it is not easy to walk along it. Here and there, walls rise up then give way to tall banks of tamarisk shrubs. She stops at the edge of the beach. The sun on the ocean hurts her eyes. She listens to the peaceful, powerful surge of the breaking waves several metres below.

There is scarcely anyone on the beach. A few teenagers are playing by the water's edge: one of them occasionally dives beneath a breaking wave and reappears further out to sea, behind the crest, then he lets himself be carried along by the following wave, which hurls him on to the sand. The sound of girls shrieking is borne on the wind. Tall, agile bodies are outlined in black against the light, making their reflections in the sparkling water of the strand seem even longer. In the distance, a fisherman casts his line then plants his long rod in the sand, sits still and waits, his arms around his knees, gazing out to sea. The sun beats down. The sun, the sea, the wind pierced by the shrill cries of the seagulls, and a few diminutive human beings. Tamia sits down at the foot of the embankment beneath the villa.

A little girl, barefoot, her flimsy dress flattened against her belly and her slender thighs by the wind, walks past her, gazing at the ground. Occasionally, she picks up a piece of driftwood sculpted by the water and bleached by the salt, a shard of glass smoothed and polished by the sand, the empty pink shell of a small crab. She scrutinises each one of her treasures before placing them carefully in the plastic bag she is holding. Tamia watches her walk away.

What else should she do? To attempt to get into the villa would seem to be impossible, or too dangerous. What would be the point, in any case? Talk to Léa? Tell her that Andrès is alive? She knows she is the first person the police would question after his escape. So?

It is for Andrès to decide, she reckons. She will tell him what she knows, what she has seen. She dismisses the muddled thoughts that well up inside her; she would like to lose them far out among the waves. Léa is running towards Andrès. Léa has forgotten him, refuses to hear tell of him. Besides, she has one, perhaps two children by this man, her husband. But she leaves them to go away with Andrès. Léa would never inform the police about Andrès. No . . .

She gets up and walks the length of the sloping beach. After a short distance there is a gap in the tamarisk bushes, leaving space for a wooden gate. Steps run down to the sand. A man is standing there, facing the sea, a dog sitting at his feet. Beyond him she notices the diving-board of a swimming-pool, then she sees the big house with large bay windows protected by raw silk blinds with thin green stripes. Tamia walks by without looking up; she can feel the man gazing at her, or perhaps she is only imagining it.

21

It is late afternoon. The garage is still open. Andrès is squatting, talking to David, who is lying underneath a car. He stands up, goes to search for a tool, and places it in David's outstretched hand. He looks up and sees that Tamia is beckoning to him from the alleyway. He says a few words to David, wipes his hands on a rag and goes to join her. They do not go inside the house, they walk around the small garden, stop by the gate, and, without noticing it, they both stare down at the dry, yellow grass where a few broken toys have been left lying. When Tamia has finished speaking, they remain standing in silence for a long while.

'It's better this way,' Andrès says at last.

And, after a moment: 'Perhaps they have children, now . . .'

A few minutes pass, then: 'Tamia . . .'

Why the sudden fear?

'Yes?'

'I want to show you something.'

He drags her into the house. Yasmine is in the kitchen, little Pierre is playing on the floor beside her. She smiles at them. Andrès waits for Tamia in the dining-room, by the low dresser in the corner of the room. He shows her a photograph in a frame.

Tamia knows it well: it was taken in front of the garage, when it first opened. David has a broad smile. In front of him is Leila, aged about five or six. One hand is placed on his daughter's shoulder, the other is around Yasmine's waist; she is pregnant with Pierre and is proudly displaying her bulging stomach. It was a neighbour who took the photograph. Tamia is next to her sister, looking very beautiful. And . . .

'Who is that man?' asks Andrès.

'That's Elijah,' says Tamia.

Ever since they came here, barely two days ago, she has frequently avoided looking at this photo. Each time she walked past it, she told herself: later. A little later.

'I know that man,' says Andrès. 'I used to know him. His name wasn't Elijah.'

'Elijah,' says Tamia once again. 'That's him.'

And, as if to quell a kind of confused murmur which arises in her mind, she repeats: 'Elijah Al Mansouri.'

But Andrès says no, he knew him; he's sure of it.

'His name was Halvan,' he says. 'I don't know what his first name was, but it wasn't Elijah. Halvan, like David; it struck me when we first arrived, the name on the garage.'

'That's the name . . . That was his mother's name.'

And then, as if in angry protest, though against whom? 'You're mistaken, surely! A resemblance . . .'

Andrès shakes his head. He looks at the photograph again, studies it, puts the frame down and goes to sit on the sofa bed. His expression is vague, lost in the past. He says that there are many things that are hazy, that he remembers only with difficulty, that he feels doubtful about. And then there are other things – he doesn't know why – memories that don't necessarily seem very important, but which have remained very clear. Images that would come to mind, down there, when everything was beginning to fray and slowly dissolve into the darkness, and which he tried to cling on to. And that man there was one of them, one of those images.

He scarcely knew him. He was a 'contact' with Libya. He had joined their section shortly before the big raid, when they were all arrested. Almost all . . .

There were several groups at the time. Various factions, it was very compartmentalised, and people were suspicious. All of them in the opposition, which was more or less active. Some long-standing differences of opinion. His section – that's what they called it, a section – was, shall we say, closest to the Party. Andrès was a journalist, a special correspondent on 'social' issues, on a moderate opposition journal which was tolerated by the regime at the time.

'Does it still exist? I haven't even felt bothered to find out!'

It was reckoned necessary to reconcile these

scattered groups, not to unite them, but at least to integrate them. That, too, was complicated. The Party was growing more unified, under his leadership, of course. In the section they were more inclined to think of unity of action, coup by coup.

'Do you understand? If there were to be unity, it would derive from the campaign; it shouldn't be required initially, ideologically . . . There I am talking like . . . like I did in those days!'

Tamia says nothing. She is leaning against the window-sill, looking outside, where the evening light is glinting on the quiet little houses, but Andrès can tell from the stillness of her back and her shoulders that she is listening. He continues. He, who has been so sparing with words about his past until now, is holding forth. He describes the secret meetings, the campaigns, not actually very numerous, and hardly ever violent, apart from that attack on a main police station to try to free comrades who had been arrested the previous day – an operation that had failed, furthermore, and had resulted in people being killed.

'A vicious circle! Campaigns, repression. it

expanded, it became more radical, we had theories for this, for that . . .'

Andrès' task, beneath his cover as a journalist, was to make contact with other groups, to gradually build up a network.

'For specific objectives, specific actions, do you understand?'

He can hear the word 'specific' snap from his mouth, the past coming back to him in this way – it's Tamia's back you're talking to!

Yasmine enters the room and asks them whether they are hungry.

Supper was a half-hearted affair; their minds were deadened, and Tamia could sense Yasmine looking at her from time to time with an anxious expression on her face. She would like to be able to reassure her, but the question of Andrès continues to reverberate, this question which her own response has not dispelled: who is this man? With an effort, she smiles at Leila, who is pressing up against her, and gently lays her hand on her bare arm for a moment.

When the meal is over, Andrès goes out into the garden. Tamia helps her sister clear the table.

'Can I leave you to finish?'

'Of course,' Yasmine says. 'Go on!'

And she kisses her.

They walk along the quiet pavements, beside the sleeping gardens. The lamplights have been switched on. A man who occasionally sits at his doorstep, smoking, greets them and they reply, 'Peace be with you too,' and continue their walk, side by side. Peace . . .

'He used to work in a ministry.'

'Which one?' asks Andrès immediately.

He can hear himself interrogating her. Like a policeman.

'Commerce. Trade with foreign countries, that was his job.'

Andrès hesitated, then: 'Libya?'

'Yes,' Tamia says eventually, in a very low voice. 'Yes, it was Libya.'

They are back outside the house, where only a faint light glows from the window of David and Yasmine's bedroom. Tamia pushes open the gate and sits down on the lawn; she suddenly feels very weary. What she is about to tell Andrès is something she did at the time in a cold fury, with a determination that nothing could have deflected. Now, everything inside her protests its weariness, would prefer to forget, to stop. Stop what?

She describes the research she did, the denials from the military police when she went to make enquiries about Elijah. The threats, violent and thinly veiled, if she persisted. She talks about the employee she met one evening in a bar near the offices from which she had just been turned away for the third time, who accosted her and whom she was about to send packing when she realised that he worked for the department she had just left. She tells of the meetings she had agreed to, the information obtained, and the price paid.

'Did you sleep with him?'

Why does he ask the question? Can't a man understand? That it has nothing to do with love, that it's not the same body? She reckons Andrès must know this, he who was so close to her, beside her in the ruined house, in the mountains. She thinks of the sharp, thin night air. Here, even now, it's still warm and a little clammy. To breathe as one did there, beneath the flimsy rug, to feel the warmth of a dear, friendly body so close to you. Here they are alone, each of them alone, and weighed down, sitting side by side on the grass.

'That man . . . he might recognise you . . .'

Why does he say that? What does it matter? She feels a surge of affection for him. Men are always a bit like children, she thinks to herself, even Andrès, even he, a man who has come back from the dead. Children in whom, deep down, that core of doubt and anxiety lies dormant, always ready to reassert itself.

'No,' she says. 'I killed him.'

After a long, silent pause, he says in a very low voice, 'Forgive me.'

It no longer makes any sense. It never did. Elijah, who was already dead when she was searching for him, and that man she had killed, whom she had almost forgotten . . . but it's the action, her action, it's the knife she plunged into his ribs, towards his heart, it's the look of astonishment in his eyes . . . she could see it all again, she could feel him in her arms, it was there. And Ahmed, the dull thud of the stone on his temple, and the eyes, those eyes once more, that looked at her and that glazed over, they were there too . . . Death was everywhere, death was already there. And the most steadfast memories were wavering. Elijah had taken the name Halvan. It was him, it was his face, the way he moved, his body that she had loved, yet does she really remember? Halvan . . . If only Andrès could recall his first name! But what does it matter? What was she thinking of? Why had he not told her anything about these contacts, as Andrès calls them, about this hidden life, without her?

It's nothing, she thinks. Why so much commotion, such confusion? It's only a tiny thing of no consequence, one you can easily understand! He wanted to protect you, to leave you out of it if things went badly, nothing more. And there you are, like a woman who discovers that the man she loves has been deceiving her for ages. As if a whole part of you, which lived, which laughed, which loved, had suddenly lost its reality, had been nothing but an illusion; as if you had been dreaming, while all the time you were already dead, even though you knew nothing about it.

It's nothing, Tamia. He was not unfaithful, there was no other woman, just a secret part of his life, which he hid from you precisely because he loved you.

So why does everything seem to crumble behind her? Like sand. And in front, so much mist . . . And even here, this evening . . .?

She stands up, she walks towards the house. She goes inside. In the sitting-room, Andrès is lying down, he has not switched off the lamp. She slips off her tunic; she is naked. She asks him to look at her, at her breasts, her belly, her hips. The caress of his eyes over her shoulders. The promise of his hands. She goes to join him, rather as one might swim, exhausted, towards an island.

22

Leila looks as fresh and gay as the morning. She adjusts the straps of her satchel and lifts up her face to Tamia.

'See you this evening, my pretty eyes,' says Tamia, kissing her lightly on each cheek.

Leila laughs. Yasmine hugs her daughter and rearranges the collar of her smock. The two sisters go outside, and from the doorstep they watch Leila, who runs over to the garage, raises her forehead first to David, then, a little more diffidently, to Andrès, and dashes off into the street, where she waves gaily to them before joining two other girls.

'I often think to myself that she looks like you did when you were her age,' Yasmine says.

Tamia laughs.

'If only that could still be true!'

Yasmine can see quite clearly that this flash of cheerfulness is over too quickly.

'Are you going to leave with him?' she asks.

Tamia leans against the door-frame, her eyes gazing vacantly in the direction of the street corner where Leila went.

'I don't know. I'd like to, but . . .'

She hesitates. Should she mention what has been weighing persistently on her mind since yesterday, and throughout the night, without the warmth of Andrès' body being able to soothe her? Tell Yasmine and be rid of it? Can words remove and consume the things she wishes to forget and that keep gnawing at her like an indistinct pain, or, on the contrary, will they pinpoint and accentuate them irrevocably?

She looks up at her sister. She repeats Andrès' words on seeing the photograph, how he seemed certain that he recognised Elijah. She mentions the name, Halvan, by which he knew him and which is Elijah's mother's name, David's name. She mentions Libya. She watches Yasmine as she speaks, as if asking her to dismiss all this with a single word, with a laugh perhaps, but Yasmine is unable to do so. What she has just heard fits in with random thoughts she and David had kept at the back of their minds, with questions that used to occur to them, concerning Elijah. Things heard, suspected, insinuated, which only bothered them and that it was best to ignore.

She wraps her arms around Tamia's shoulders, tries to find calming and reassuring words. After all, she says, if Andrès is right, if Elijah was involved in secret activities, it would explain the reasons for his arrest and disappearance, which have never really been understood. Why did he allow you to remain in ignorance? To protect you, no doubt.

Tamia says nothing. Yasmine's arm and body press happily and warmly against her. Between her and the doubts, the fears. A lassitude, a vague, aimless sadness. She longs to curl up here, where the world is calm and certain. She rests her hand on top of Yasmine's, which is placed on her own shoulder.

The silver bracelet gleams softly on her bare forearm. She remembers that temptation which came over her on several occasions down there: to stay with the old woman, to remain among the silence of the mountains and allow time to flow peacefully by.

She sits up straight and Yasmine gently removes her arm. Over there, by the garage door, David is talking to Andrès, who is listening to him, his head bowed, rolling a pebble mechanically with the tip of his shoe.

'David may have something for him,' says Yasmine. 'A man he knows slightly, an Italian involved in smuggling, who may be able to get him out of the country.'

Tamia watches the two men. She no longer knows.

23

'I CAN SEE HIM THIS EVENING,' SAYS David. 'With you, if you'd like.'

Andrès says yes, of course, without looking up. But what about the cost? This man surely doesn't do it for nothing.

David speaks softly, weighing his words. He says that he has talked about it to Yasmine. In order to build the garage, they used the mother's legacy, half of which was left to Tamia and which they must repay her. If she agrees . . .

Andrès nods, without taking his eyes off the ground.

'I'm going . . . I'm going to take a walk,' he says after a moment's silence. 'To think. We'll see the man this evening.'

He wanders off without looking at David, who reckons that this business about the money embarrasses him.

'Be careful!' he says.

And he goes back towards the garage, to the car that awaits him and from which he must remove the engine. He has already stripped it of parts, and he is securing it to the chains of a hoist that hang from the garage roof. Each of his movements is precise, born of professional experience. There is a joy to be had in watching hands that know what they are doing, that select the necessary tool without any hesitation.

He grabs hold of the bit of chain hanging from the hoist, and he starts to pull steadily, one hand after the other. Inch by inch the engine extricates itself from the car, and with each tug of the arms the hoist makes its clicking noise, that metallic song he loves to hear, which echoes through the quiet neighbourhood. The reassuring noise of a garage.

24

Andrès did not go back to the house; he made his way directly to the street, and Tamia can see him as he walks away in the direction of the town. As she watches him disappear, she restrains her longing to call out to him, to run after him, and she slowly turns away. She stifles her fear, the thoughts that besiege her. She avoids the kitchen, where Yasmine is busy; she goes and sits down in the drawing-room, on the sofa they use as their bed. She sits very straight, her hands on her knees, her gaze lost in a large photograph of the desert that decorates the wall facing her. Vast dunes on which the setting sun sculpts sharp ridges. Yellow ochre sand,

and a sky of an intense, uniform blue. She is alone.

Andrès walks through the town. He passes the building that serves as premises for the newspaper for which he once worked, and he is amazed to find so few changes. The same flower shop and the same café flanking the entrance, where the same doorman, wearing his customised uniform, keeps watch. No, this is an old man too, but he's not the same one. As a precaution, however, Andrès makes a detour.

Now he walks down towards the port. He is no longer used to towns: he has to be careful crossing roads, even stepping off the pavement; all those actions that were once second nature to him and which he now has to think about. They take his mind off the task he has set himself: to see what is going on at 'that place' for himself. They distract him, and so much the better, for he prefers to remain in this state of vagueness.

He veers off towards the beach, goes down to the water's edge, where the waves lap and where the sand is firmer beneath his feet. A few early-morning fishermen are casting their lines;

it is the time of day when the bass lurk around the sandbanks. He occasionally halts close to one of them, watches him slowly reel in his line, pull it in and examine it, then cast off again with a flowing motion. He follows the trajectory of the bait, which plunges into the water, out beyond the rollers, waits for a moment, then the fisherman begins again.

Higher up, a hundred metres or so away, begin the dunes that lead up to the large white villas. He tries to recognise the one Tamia had described to him: the thuja hedge, the wooden gate, the man and the dog. They all look alike. This one, perhaps? But she mentioned a swimming-pool . . . Then this one? But there's a low stone wall that separates it from the beach . . . He walks on like this, watching from the corners of his eyes.

In the distance there is a man, a curious insect on the white sand. He is throwing a stick into the waves and a large black dog tirelessly fetches it and brings it back to him. Andrès stops; he looks out to sea. The man and the dog are walking up towards the dunes. The steps, the gate, that's the place.

25

He is sitting in the sand, with his back resting against the dune. Far enough away not to be considered suspicious by the man in black who is evidently guarding the house. The sun is already high in the sky; the light offshore breeze ruffles the air that is now burning hot, occasionally creating a little eddy of sand and dried seaweed. The seagulls that cried as they flew over his head are sporadic now.

A very old man clad in a white dressing gown comes out of the house next door. He stops a few yards away from Andrès, removes his gown, which he folds carefully and lays on the sand with his sandals, and then walks down to the sea. His swimming trunks hang on him.

He is unbelievably thin: his bones protrude beneath his flabby skin, and there are no longer any muscles in his bowed legs, which nevertheless carry him hesitantly, but without faltering. He walks into the sea at the same pace until all that can be seen is his head with its few white hairs that merge with the foam. Then he turns around, returns at the same pace and walks back to his dressing-gown. A tortoise, Andrès thinks, an old tortoise, hard nose, emaciated neck. All tortoises are old!

The old man has now gone back inside his house. At no time did he look at Andrès.

How can anyone live, as old as that, in a body that has almost disappeared, a frame so weak, fragile and wasted? What can they smell of the heat of the sun, the coolness of the sea? Of the fragrances and the sounds of a world they should already have left behind, which they will soon leave? What are they still waiting for, other than death, which has already taken possession of the wrinkled skin and the brown marks that overrun it, in this sparsely shrouded skeleton?

He was like that, it suddenly occurs to him. Almost as thin, almost as feeble. He examines his hands, dry and brown. He remembers his pallid skin, the stench of rotting flesh. And what had he been waiting for in his hole – he too – apart from death?

And what is he waiting for now, sitting with his arms around his folded knees, alone on the burning sand?

Thoughts rise up, they pass and vanish like puffs of wind. Then all that remains, behind his misty eyes, behind his eyelids and their constant, weary blinking, is a desert of sand where a part of him, still alive, waits without hope, waits nevertheless. Waits for the appearance over there, at the wooden gate between the thujas, of the woman who so quickly forgot him.

The sun is already setting. High above, the wind combs some clouds that he had not noticed before into long, broken wisps. He stands up, though why at that particular moment? A kind of signal, whose meaning he does not understand, which prompts his body to move, makes him go down to the sea once more, then to walk along the beach in the direction of the port.

A crowd of noisy, bustling children blocks

his path. He approaches, leans over them to look at the object of their excitement. It is the body of a small, beached dolphin, lying on its side. Its skin is dark and shiny, where the waves still wash over it, but death, dry and grey, has spread over the rest of its corpse, over the white, puckered and apparently empty belly, that reminds him of an old man's body. The head lies there, weary and abandoned; the half-open mouth remains poised between a last cry or a last smile. The eye socket is dark and hollow: flies are crawling out, burrowing in. With the help of a stick, a child lifts the tail out of the water with difficulty, and allows it to fall back with a soft, thudding sound. A little girl laughs, a sickening laugh. He walks away.

He does not go back through the centre of town, but skirts round via the outlying districts, the industrial zones with their dusty pavements littered with greasy papers, plastic bags and oil-covered debris. The workers have already left; only an old woman hangs around, picking up a rag here and there, or a bottle, which she inspects as she mutters something before tossing it into the supermarket trolley she wheels in front of her. A little further on lies a district of dilapidated buildings, almost a shanty town, where children with hungry, feverish eyes and women with hard, ugly, ruined faces look at him with mistrust. And suddenly there is the charming sight of two very young girls, laughing, with teeth like pearls and long, flowing black hair that almost touches the ground, who give him the most fleeting of glances – did they even see him? – before vanishing into a hovel.

A few streets more, and the huts with corrugated-iron roofs give way to small houses, the pavements are clean and made of cement, there are flowers in the tiny gardens, and cars in front of the gates. Cheerful children, and slightly less ugly women at the open kitchen windows. And men raking the gravel paths, or painting their fences. Andrès' footsteps become slower, a sudden weariness makes his legs feel heavy. He is approaching the house of David and Yasmine, the house where Tamia awaits him. Where the man who may be able to help him leave the country is due to arrive shortly.

Tamia greets him without a smile. She reaches out to him with her lips, he takes her in his arms; he can feel that her body is heavy, like his. Her face, too, is tired, and the two lines that frame her mouth are furrowed, two indications of suffering that incise themselves in the core of Andrès' breast. She does not ask him any questions.

'The man is already here,' she says, nodding in the direction of the garage.

26

'It'll be in three days' time, or else in a month,' the Italian had said.

It is only at the new moon that they dare take the risk: the coastguards here do not have radar at their disposal and are unable to detect them. Andrès, whose eyes are wide open in the darkness and who is lying beside Tamia, does not say when he will leave, and she does not ask him.

She lies still and is tense; he can sense this and puts his hand on her arm. The night slips by, pitch-black and silent. A little later, as if calling for help:

'Andrès . . .'

He squeezes her hand. Hesitantly to begin

with, the words that have been held back for hours begin to pour out. Is there anyone who may know more about Elijah? That assumed name, Libya . . . Is there anyone . . . ?

He pauses. Possibly, he says eventually. Perhaps at the newspaper, if he still works there, a man who was his friend, who knew all about these matters, who had links with the networks. Perhaps he knew what happened afterwards, after the arrest of Andrès and his friends? But he cannot get in touch with him, it would be too dangerous, he could not be sufficiently sure of the man to disclose his presence here.

'I can go and find him,' she said. 'Naturally, I won't refer to you. I'll try to find out what happened . . . "People" have mentioned his name . . .'

'Possibly,' Andrès says again. 'If he's still there!'

She asks him the name again, he tells her, she can sense his reluctance.

A few minutes go by, then Andrès says, 'He knew my brother, Jan, too. They did a story together, in Bosnia. Perhaps you can give his name as a reference, say that it was he who gave you his name . . .'

They stop talking. They remain awake for a long time. The light touch of Andrès' fingers on the silver bracelet is their only contact.

Early next morning, she calls the newspaper. The man in question still works there, she can speak to him a little later. Andrès, who is sitting with his elbows planted on the kitchen table, listens, says nothing. Tamia comes to join him, sits down beside him, and Yasmine anxiously asks them if they would like some more coffee. Familiar sounds come from the garage; David is already at work.

Tamia strokes little Pierre's head; he is still in his pyjamas. She gazes at him without really seeing him; the child grows restless, turns away from her and goes and clings to his mother's legs. Yasmine asks him what he wants; he doesn't know.

'I'll go there,' says Tamia, getting to her feet. 'I'll be available, if he can see me immediately.'

She goes to get dressed. It occurs to Andrès that he ought to follow her, but he does not move. In his restless early morning sleep he had a dream that he is trying to recall and that continues to evade him, a pointless pursuit from which he is unable to extricate himself.

He drinks his coffee, which is lukewarm now, and looks up at Tamia, who comes over to kiss him. Their gazes meet and part. He follows her with his eyes until she disappears behind the hedge of the house next door.

He gets to his feet, goes out and stands on the doorstep. He breathes in the still chilly morning air; he would like to fill his chest completely but is unable to do so properly. He takes a few steps towards the garage, pauses, stops. He can feel Yasmine looking at him – on his back, on his shoulders – from the kitchen window; he stands still. Then he looks around: the window is empty.

He proceeds down the path as far as the gate; he opens it, he is in the street. A slow walk to begin with, then his pace quickens. He takes the route he took the previous day in the opposite direction, towards the shanty towns and the industrial zone, towards the beach.

27

Tamia replaces the receiver and leaves the telephone kiosk. Half past twelve, the man had said, at the café near the newspaper office. Over two hours to wait. She walks the streets as her fancy takes her, without straying too far from the centre. The town bustles about in the rising heat. Faces with expressions that are busy, anxious, generally hard, occasionally sad. Streams of lethal cars. Beaches with foul stenches.

A square with dust-covered trees. She sits down on one of the two concrete benches. A woman who turns her back to her is seated at the other one. The woman has surrounded herself with several bags which she dips into occasionally and pulls out some indecipherable object, which she stares at for some time, before putting it away again. When she is not busying herself with this little game, the woman stares at a large shop window on the other side of the railings of the square. It is a luxurious shop, with pushchairs, prams, toys and children's clothes. A collection of pinkish-white plastic dolls, their heads bare, has been assembled in the window, a fearsome assortment of simulated children that look identical and terrifying.

From behind, the woman is stocky and of indeterminate age. When she turns her head to busy herself with one of her bags, Tamia is amazed to see a face that still looks young.

A sad, yellow dog comes to sniff at the bags, then turns away and approaches Tamia at a slanting trot. She holds out her hand to it, but the dog shies away and goes off, baring its teeth.

Still another hour. She thinks of the questions she will put to the man. On the telephone he sounded kindly, but reserved, cautious.

'Jan Aslegg, yes, I know him well. I'm not sure I can help you,' he had said. 'No, don't give me details, you can tell me later.'

She stands up. Gazes briefly again at the

woman who is absorbed in her stubborn back-and-forth motion: the bag, then a long gaze at the window. The bag, the window . . .

She leaves the square, checks her watch and drifts away into the town that blares around her.

28

YASMINE HAS GONE DOWN TO THE garage. David, seeing her approaching, stands up and smiles at her.

'That woman . . .' says Yasmine. 'Andrès was a prisoner, and she . . . so quickly! Barely a year . . .'

David wipes his hands on a rag.

'She believed him to be dead,' he says.

Without conviction, for all he wants to do is to calm Yasmine, he adds without knowing why, 'So did we, after a year, without any news; we certainly thought Elijah was dead . . . And we were right!'

'Not Tamia,' says Yasmine. 'Tamia didn't believe that! Even if she was wrong . . .'

29

Andrès is sitting down, his back to the slope, in the same place as the previous day. His legs folded, his arms around his knees. The same position as when he was in the well, the same difficulty, the same pain when he decides to stand up. How long has he been there now? The beach has become a little more lively, it must be midday. A few fishermen are pulling in their lines and walking away in the direction of the port. A group of teenagers is swimming over there, their youthful laughter carried on the breeze, mingled with the mocking cries of the seagulls.

He walks down to the water's edge, rolls up his trouser legs, leaves his sandals on the sand

and enters the sea, stopping when it washes over his ankles. The sensation of cold lasts only a moment and recedes, except when a more powerful wave reaches his calves. Beneath his feet, the ebb of the tide makes him sink deeper into the sand with each surge and he wonders whether he could gradually bury himself completely were he to stay there long enough. He would probably look semi-beached, rather like the dolphin he saw yesterday. Children would find him like that, lying on one side, his head resting on the sand. He thinks of the dolphin's empty eyes, of the insects in the hollow sockets. 'Crows and magpies, we have hollowed-out eyes . . .' Here, there are the seagulls, and the flies.

Hollowed-out: a dull, flat ring, a whiff of mildew, a pale dampness in the dark, here, beneath the noonday sun . . .

A movement on the strand makes him look up from his feet, which are gradually being covered with sand: the large black dog is galloping around the beach in crazy circles, passing a few feet away from him and returning to the man in black over there who is calling to it. And, at the foot of the steps, a tall figure wearing a dress that reaches her ankles and makes her look even taller; it is she.

She, standing tall in the wind that moulds the flimsy material to her belly, to her thighs. She raises her arms to tie back her hair, which is longer than it used to be, Andrès reflects, and her breasts begin to hurt his eyes; then his hands remember.

Beside her, a very small child totters unsteadily on the sand, his arms stretched out, drawing him towards the sea which his impatient hands think they can already touch. The dog comes and nuzzles him, possibly giving him a lick in the process, for the child has his eyes shut and falls on the sand in a seated position, covering his face and clumsily trying to protect it even though the dog has already gone away. She laughs.

She laughs. She takes the child in her outstretched arms and lifts him up level with her eyes, a little higher even, for she has to toss her head back, and she gazes at him as you would gaze at the sun; she holds him as you would hold the sun in your hands if you were a mother or a priestess and were on familiar terms with God.

Andrès' head drops.

He emerges from the water. He gathers up his sandals, which he will carry in his hands. He disappears in the direction of the port, an anonymous, insignificant walker. He does not look back.

30

'WERE YOU NOT SUSPICIOUS?' ASKS THE man sitting opposite Tamia at a table in the rear of the restaurant, a place where he suggested they sit because it is less noisy and more secluded.

Tamia shakes her head. She has not touched the salad she ordered, whereas the man eats heartily and takes great swigs of beer. He is warm and friendly. Initially reserved, he has been happy to answer Tamia's questions.

'Suspicious . . . of what?'

That he was involved in a secret operation? Yes, in some ways. His absences, the trips to Libya, a certain secretiveness, yes, she could be suspicious of that, even if she did not ask him questions.

'I loved him,' she said by way of explanation.

Words that are uttered in a low, flat voice, which she can hear as they drift into the confused babble of the restaurant.

It is true: she was not really surprised when he was arrested. There had been no grounds for indictment in his dossier at the military police – she did not say how she had found out – only that he had been transferred to Achkent. Without trial, without sentence.

'But these things you are saying . . . Are you sure?'

'Yes,' he said. 'We had our suspicions to begin with, and then the proofs. Two years ago, perhaps, after a wave of arrests that caused a furore, an entire group of opponents was broken up. That's when we knew that they had been shopped by Halvan, who had infiltrated them; Halvan, whose real name was Elijah Al Mansouri. Who had already freed a number of illegal resistance fighters, over several years. And who, in fact, had also disappeared himself. We deduced that he had gone into hiding in order to escape eventual reprisals.'

*

Both of them are silent. The man looks at Tamia. With bowed head, she is absent-mindedly turning over the salad with the tip of her fork. A sort of vague rumble in her head is trying to deaden the cruel, biting thoughts that impose themselves nonetheless. Elijah was a double agent, a traitor. Over several years . . . Andrès, who had recognised his photograph, who suspected him, never said so openly, but now she understands. Elijah, who was sweet and gentle with her. Elijah, for whom she had searched so far beyond the mountains . . .

She raises her head, looks at the man. She says there is one thing she does not understand: if Elijah was in the pay of the police, why did they send him to prison, and no doubt mistreat him, since he died there very soon after his arrival?

The man does not ask her how she knows this. An image, a thought, occurs to him as he observes her face, as he scans those two delicate, clear lines that have just vanished from the corners of her mouth: she is made of a very hard crystal, which is susceptible to minute cracks. He says that it surprises him too, that perhaps the police had wanted to rid themselves in this way of an informer whose cover had been blown and who was becoming an embarrassment. These things happen. He says that he may possibly reopen the dossier and riffle through it a bit. Where can he get in touch with her, if he has anything to impart?

'I'll come here tomorrow at midday,' she says. 'And the following days as well. You know where to find me.'

He does not push the matter any further. He summons the waiter, pays and stands up. He lays his hand on Tamia's, which does not move. Then he leaves. The waiter asks whether he should remove the salad that she has not touched. Yes, she says.

31

In the burning afternoon sun that lulls the town, Tamia and Andrès return to the house by two different routes, slowly and with difficulty. She arrives home first, and Yasmine, who has seen her coming, goes to the front door to greet her. There is something damaged, broken, in the weary gait with which Tamia walks up the gravel path, in her face that is unable to smile. Yasmine asks no questions of her and both of them sit down side by side on the doorstep, in the shade of the house.

Something has to be done . . . This is all that Tamia can think of: something. What? Gather up and piece together everything that is unravelling, such as her thoughts, and find the energy to do so? But it is weariness that prevails: things are losing their clarity of outline, their brightness of colour; the world is turning grey and blurring over, and even her sister's touch, the hip and shoulder she can feel against her, and this arm that is not sure whether to put itself round her, are to no avail. No more than the arrival of Andrès, who stops to look at them from the garden gate.

Neither is Andrès able to catch and hold Tamia's gaze or rest his eyes in hers; as she looks up at him his eyes are already avoiding hers, and everything splits in two and divides and drifts away and disappears with the relentless slow pace of galaxies. Yasmine is suddenly and inexplicably frightened and pricks up her ears: wasn't that little Pierre waking up from his siesta, didn't he call her? But there is only silence in the house. And, fortunately, the distant clinking of a tool that David has dropped on the cement floor, over there in the garage.

That evening, without having managed to speak to one another, they make love, desperately. Their bodies refuse to respond to the pleasure, try to rediscover one another, fail to do so, persist, then give up and, side by side, without touching , they let their sweat dry over their naked, disconsolate, forsaken skin.

'He must leave,' says David. 'It's dangerous. For him, for us. And then . . .'

He does not finish. Yasmine says nothing.

'The day after tomorrow,' David continues.

He can see from the green numbers on the alarm clock that it is past midnight.

'No. Tomorrow!'

32

THE FOLLOWING DAY, THE MAN DID NOT come to the restaurant. Tamia waited for him for over an hour, then she left.

The woman and the child did not go out. Only the man and his dog appeared; the man looked briefly in Andrès' direction, then let his dog loose on the beach, after which they returned home.

Mackerel clouds swept across the sky during the afternoon. There may be rain tonight.

33

TODAY, THE MAN HAS KEPT THE rendezvous. From the table at which she is sitting, the one they occupied the first day, Tamia, who arrived early, can see him coming towards her. He sits down, he avoids her gaze, he asks whether she has ordered anything. He still does not know whether he should tell her what he has discovered, and has had verified, since he would prefer it to be incorrect. Because it seems to him that he has been the instigator of an absurd and deadly farce; because sometimes, particularly today, he loathes his job, which prides itself on serving the truth and only succeeds in stirring up shreds of misery on top of blood and filth. Because he feels guilty about what he is about to say, about what he is about to do to him.

Of course it is excessive, he tells himself; he is only the messenger, it is not his fault! And better cruelty than the putrefaction of lies. Excessive and suspect, and it's been exaggerated in order to suppress it. Suppress what? Why, when he opens his mouth to speak, does he think of the murder of a child?

He has made enquiries, he says. Obtained information, which he has had confirmed by other sources. He holds back on the details, delays the moment. Tamia knows and can feel this. Oddly enough she is not impatient, she has no idea what he is going to say to her, but she is almost grateful to him for dragging out the time in this way, like a respite, a reprieve before the execution. Besides, what more can he disclose to her beyond what he has already told her? A few shabby details? She has imagined every one of them. Not this one.

Elijah is alive, the man says. He is in Syria, under a new identity. He is leading a prosperous life. It is another man who was sent, using his name, to Achkent, and who died there.

34

THE MAN WITH THE DOG MADE A BRIEF appearance. He spent a few minutes standing at the gate, without going down to the beach, then he called to his dog and vanished.

It is overcast today: the fluffy clouds of the previous day have thickened into a layer of uniform grey, but it has not rained. There is not the slightest breath of wind. On the sea there are the merest ripples of waves that come from very far out and only curl and foam at the point at which they break over the shingle. Their muffled breathing protracts time. The confused and troubled thoughts of men – of Andrès, the man who is sitting there with his back to the dunes – will have been dispersed a long time ago, will have been of no more importance, no more substance than the transient gleam made on the sand by the surge of the wave as it ebbs away; the sea will continue to rumble, peaceful and powerful, when there is no one there to hear it.

Today, doubtless, she will not come. He speaks her name, Léa, in a low voice, as if he were trying to resuscitate this dead thing inside him, this ember which is no longer memory yet which refuses to fade away.

What are you waiting for? What are you looking for? What is it that brings you back here, doggedly, without hope, without desire? Think of the power of those torturers who left their mark on you for ever, who did not just dig down into the ground to make a hole into which to cast your body, but delved into your head so as to entomb your mind! Get out . . .

Is it her you are waiting for? Is it her you want to return to? You can no longer even remember her. That pang of excitement in your hands, when she tied back her hair, when she lifted up her child like an offering, when her body stood out against the sky and her breasts made your eyes pop out, was that a memory?

Memories are alive, they permit caresses, arouse nostalgic affection, gently arouse desire; they know how to relinquish it and help it survive, or truly perish. Was that a memory?

He thinks of a man who was dying. Whom he saw cut down in his zeal by a bullet, shattered as he was fleeing by an invisible gunman. With the help of his photographer, he pulled him from the shelter of the ruined wall, just where they had taken refuge themselves. A young man, whose hands were clutching at the hole in his chest. The blood welled up between his fingers in a steady flow that grew gradually weaker. Those wide-open eyes glued to his, what did they see in his eyes? And a word, the same one, barely articulated by his lips as they were turning blue, a foreign word, which he could not understand. One that grew slowly softer as the source of his blood ran dry. A name, that of a woman perhaps. The word died with him, he died with the word; they accompanied one another till the end.

In the mountains, the soldier's mouth was also open as the blood from his head, smashed by the stone, poured out. It was open, but no word, no name was spoken. He was looking at Tamia.

A large ship passes in the distance, slowly tracing the blurred line of the horizon. From right to left, towards the past, thinks Andrès, who remembers that as a child that was how he drew time passing.

You know what it is that keeps you rooted here, what binds you and fascinates you: betrayal, that claw reaching out from the past. What betrayal? Léa's? It's nothing. Did you love one another so much? Besides, she believed you were dead, she wanted to live. You yourself, and without that excuse, have fallen in love with Tamia, you still love her, she alone has become real and alive for you. So, what betrayal?

He does not know. Perhaps he should think about it further, should complete his research, like the ship out there which steams steadily on, without faltering, towards that mingled patch of sea and sky. Perhaps he should. This evening, another ship awaits him. He must not miss it.

He leans on one arm to raise himself, and it is then that he sees the soldiers. A compact line of a dozen or so men coming towards him from the direction of the port. And as he turns his head, one knee on the ground, ready to escape, he sees the other line of soldiers, on the opposite side, who have emerged from the path that runs alongside the villa. The soldiers converge on him, those nearest the sea are walking more quickly, tightening the net of their camouflage battledress. Up there, at the top of the steps, the man holds the black dog by the leash and watches. She is not there, Andrès reckons, and he sits down again and waits for them.

35

'Perhaps he'll go directly there?' says David.

That morning he had reminded him of the time, and the place: the old deconsecrated cemetery, at the far end of the port. That is where they would leave from, at one o'clock in the morning.

He does not really believe what he is saying. Andrès will not leave.

'Perhaps,' says Tamia.

She is floating, disconnected. Entire walls are crumbling, successive strata of life that were nothing but delusions are collapsing one after the other, it will never stop, there is nothing to discover, nothing to grab and cling on to, no solid ground in which to take root at last. Elijah was no longer there, he was dead, it was not him. Elijah was not Elijah and he is not dead. Nightmares, and each awakening, far from releasing him, gives way to another nightmare. The world is losing its substance, and she herself is becoming transparent, illusory. Even Andrès . . .

Andrès, however . . .

His arms, his hands, his smell, however. They are still there. A little.

'Perhaps,' she says again, more resolutely. 'Perhaps he has gone into hiding until his departure. We can't be sure, we must go down there. I'll go and get his bag ready.'

On the sitting-room table she carefully folds a few clothes; with slow deliberation she smoothes the creases of the shirts and the pair of trousers, as if she were giving a farewell caress, and she finds it increasingly hard to take her hand away. She arranges them in the bag, which she closes before checking its weight; it is light and will not impede him. She looks at her watch: it is only eleven o'clock.

36

He does not feel the blows that continue to rain down on him; he no longer hears the questions – always the same ones – that are yelled at him.

'Who helped you?'

'How did you get out?'

'Was the soldier an accessory?'

'It was you who killed him!'

'Where were you, all these months, since your escape?'

He can no longer feel the heavy truncheon blows on his head, on his back, on his crushed and lifeless hands. A moment ago, a more violent blow had broken something in his chest – he knew it had. Since then, a kind of peace has come over him, a strange enclave in the midst of the rage and the shouting, in the belly of this concrete cellar lit by bare light-bulbs. One of them, smashed by a truncheon, is swaying; he recognises it, it is out of Guernica, and he laughs like a dying horse. A furious blow to the mouth shatters his teeth.

Tamia. Tamia's back and her broad shoulders and her sweet hips, by the fountain, they are what he must cling on to.

Slowly – there is no sadness – they begin to fade. A thin circle of light still, up there, which is growing dimmer. And his mouth with its ruptured lips will laugh one last time, because now he can see, he can hold, that moment he has striven for so much and which has always escaped him, the moment when the light, all of a sudden, is extinguished.

37

In the ink-black night they can hear the ship as it sails away. A muffled, regular throbbing sound that penetrates the night, the invisible rocks and trees, and even their own breasts and their guts. And which never stops fading away.

Which will eventually fade away, without anyone having been able to detect the precise moment it disappeared.

'He didn't come,' says David.

'He's dead,' says Tamia.

38

In very slow, perfect circles the storks soar above the village. Perched on its long, rusty legs, the old water tank stands out against the still-luminous sky in a sunset bruised by a thin band of clouds. A gradual alchemy continues gently to transform the mountain, to despatch it into the night. The blue hills are already mauve here, and very dark now that the ridges are carved out against the sky. The blue-green of the cedars dissolves without growing any darker until they blend into the valley. The trail of clouds which a moment ago was bursting with reds and oranges is, when she looks up, nothing now but a trace in which the pink is turning grey and growing pale. And while she walks around the village, without any other purpose than to rediscover, stone by stone, the path by which they had left, the storks, one by one, forsake their peaceful orbits and return to their nests.

At a steady pace, she walks up through the scattered rocks and the gentle layers of cropped grass. As she climbs higher up the mountain the air grows cooler and lighter, in steadily increasing layers. The slope is entirely in shadow, and she cannot see the ruins of the hamlet, but a thin column of smoke rises vertically into the sky above the ridge. And as she approaches, the donkey greets her three times with a noise that resembles a wail or a call.

She stops by the enclosure and strokes its nose and velvet muzzle. A few more steps and the old woman is waiting for her on her doorstep, her dark silhouette outlined against the warm yellow light of her oil lamp. Tamia lets the bag hanging from her shoulder slip to the ground and walks over to her. The old woman holds out both her hands, palms upwards, as if she were receiving some gift or making an offering, and Tamia takes them in hers.

Without speaking, each of them gazes at their conjoined hands: Tamia's strong, young hands, the fingers of which linger on the very soft, wrinkled skin of the old woman's wrist. And after a little while the woman removes her gnarled and deformed fingers that have been stroking Tamia's forearm and places them, almost timidly, on the silver bracelet. They remain there for a brief second, time for a very quick smile. A young girl's smile, a memory, barely glimpsed in the flickering light of the lamp.

* OLD WOMAN
AND YOUNG TAMIA
SAME PEOPLE / PERSON

2 AGES OF ONE PERSON
AT THE SAME TIME

TIES - MAN LEAVING (ALONE)
PLACE ...
DONKEY + WHO PAID
BRACELET

www.vintage-books.co.uk